More praise
and
THE GOOD FIGHT

"Matera takes on social and moral issues. She also delivers the goods a mystery writer should, with intelligence, humor, and gutsy femininity."
Robert Campbell

"An engaging heroine who may never return to the dusty confines of a law library."
St. Louis Post-Dispatch

"By any standard this is superior murder fiction. The author's sensitive depiction of the fall-out from Vietnam and the Sixties adds a poignant quality to a detective story with more than ordinary dimension, featuring a heroine who is warm, capable, tough and appealingly feminine. Skillfully plotted, expertly written . . . its story compelling and satisfying, as befits all first-rate writing."
Mostly Murder

"More proof that some of the leanest, most tough-minded prose is coming from women . . . With emotional zingers throughout and no easy answers."
The Kirkus Reviews

Also by Lia Matera:

HIDDEN AGENDA
THE SMART MONEY*
A RADICAL DEPARTURE
WHERE LAWYERS FEAR TO TREAD*

Forthcoming from Ballantine Books

THE GOOD FIGHT

A Laura Di Palma Mystery

Lia Matera

BALLANTINE BOOKS • NEW YORK

Copyright © 1990 by Lia Matera

All rights reserved under International and Pan-American Copyright Conventions, including the right of reproduction in whole or in part in any form. Published in the United States of America by Ballantine Books, a division of Random House, Inc., New York, and simultaneously in Canada by Random House of Canada Limited, Toronto.

Library of Congress Catalog Card Number: 89-28112

ISBN 0-345-37107-0

This edition published by arrangement with Simon and Schuster, Inc.

Manufactured in the United States of America

First Ballantine Books Edition: May 1991

To
Maura Matera, Judy Greber, and Marilyn Wallace, with love; and to Dominick Abel and Steve Padgitt, with thanks.

PROLOGUE

Hal Di Palma climbed out of bed. It took awhile. His right leg was rubbery and unresponsive. He could raise his right arm and rotate it, open and close his hand. The hand still tingled and his fingers didn't register the texture of objects he touched. He had to look at them to make sure he gripped objects with sufficient force to keep them from sliding out of his fist. But that was okay. Nothing anybody else would notice.

He felt his way across the room. Near the partially open door, a trapezoid of linoleum glinted with soft fluorescent light. He could see no one in the corridor. His room was far from the check-in desk and reception-area couches. It was near the kitchen; he heard the clatter of trays several times a day. Not now; he'd managed to waken long before breakfast.

He closed himself into the bathroom and turned on the light above the mirror, a sheet of institutional metal that made his skin look purplish. His hair stuck up in sleepy patches. He was surprised to see so much white in it. He remembered its being mostly black. The rest of him looked as bad as he'd expected.

His eyes were red and watery, especially his right eye. At the veterans hospital (God, sixteen years ago?) it had been months before the eyelid closed properly. How many months would it be this time?

In addition, everything on the right side of his face was a little off. The right cheek seemed hollower than the left, the corner of his mouth drooped a little. Hal rubbed the stubble on his chin. The right side felt a little numb still.

He pulled open the cabinet and looked inside. A cordless electric razor. He'd looked earlier and discovered this object, but hadn't been quite sure what it was. Now, thank God, he recognized it.

He'd never used a cordless razor before. He fumbled with it interminably before finally hitting the ''on'' button. The sudden buzzing startled him so that he almost dropped it in the sink. Then he jerked the contoured head over his chin.

He washed, his right hand failing to cup the water so that he splashed it over his pajamas and onto the floor. He wet his hair and fingercombed it back off his face.

He searched his eyes intently in the mirror, trying to reassure himself that he was still the same man: thirty-seven, reasonably strong, emotionally tough. But Jesus, he looked scary. Gaunt and angry. He recalled a dark, smelly bar somewhere in the Southwest, a crazy husk of a drunkard who kept slamming money on the table and bellowing, ''I got me a dollar says I can whip any man in the place!''

Disconcerted by the physical resemblance, Hal turned away.

Getting his clothes out of the cupboard was tricky in the dark. Getting himself into them was even trickier. The trek across the small room had knocked the stuffing out of him. It was hard to shuck pajama shirt and trousers, to bend and lift his limbs into stiffer, less-yielding clothes.

Hal lay back on the bed for a few minutes when he was done, his heart hammering and his skin clammy from exertion. His mouth tasted sour. He'd forgotten to brush his teeth, but the bathroom seemed miles away, and the necessary movements—holding the brush, squeezing the tube, scrubbing the teeth, even spitting so that he didn't spot his sweater—seemed far beyond him.

He heard footsteps in the corridor, and because he had to, he found the energy and coordination to push back the bedsheet and then pull it over himself, all the way up to his neck to hide his cable-knit sweater.

He'd barely finished when a nurse said, "Uh oh—woke you up."

They were so damn cheerful at this place. It was like being locked up in a department store.

"That's okay," he croaked.

She smiled. "Boy, you're sure making fast . . ." something. Progress, he guessed. She said something else that slid in and out of his consciousness without reaching his understanding. She tapped the plastic bottle hooked to the side of his bed.

"No." His voice was hoarse with irritation. If he had to make a wish right now it would be never again to pee into a bottle held by a stranger. He felt nauseous, the desire was so fervent.

She nodded and smiled again, then held up a tiny white Dixie cup. "Medication time."

Damn. If he sat up, she'd see the clothes.

He forced his head forward and opened his mouth.

Simultaneously she offered the cup and her arm, to raise him. With his lips and tongue, he tipped the pills into his mouth and swallowed them, opening again to show her they were gone.

The nurse was clearly startled. "Gosh. Let me get you some water."

He wasn't actually sure she'd said water, but it made sense that way. "No water," he replied.

The pills stuck in his throat and he barely kept down the contents of his stomach. He was so damn tired. More than tired, stressed. Hot with sweat, scared. He wondered, with an edge of panic, what the pills did. Would they make him pass out somewhere? Worse yet, were they keeping him alive? Would he have some kind of attack without them?

He tried to reassure himself. Think of the pharmacopoeia they'd stuffed down his gullet at the veterans hospital. Everything from antibiotics to antipsychotics. No wonder he'd lain there like a vegetable for the better part of a year.

Without that shit he'd been able to get by in the world. Not exactly prosper, but get by. Pass for a human being.

And this latest affliction was just some kind of seizure. Caused by—what? He remembered waking up to a mouthful of carpet. He didn't remember how he got there. Hit from behind?

Whatever the hell happened, it wasn't a bullet in the brain like last time. How bad off could he be?

The nurse gave a cheery wave and left the room.

He told himself he'd better wait until she finished her rounds, but he knew why he was lying there. Jesus, if a wash and a shave took this much out of him, how the hell was he going to make it outside?

He thought of places he'd called home—a rusted-out old van, a windy stretch of beach, every kind of woodland from sugar maple to mangrove to sodden evergreen. He'd make it the way he always made it.

For a split second, a sensory trick brought him the smell of oiled wood walls and backyard gully: his boyhood room. He lay still, weathering the memory—the memory and all its associations: his mother carping at him to invite her doctor's son to dinner, his father buying him that mortifying sports car, his picture in the paper every time he won a fucking swimming certificate or spelling bee.

Comfort didn't make a place home. Comfort was a cattle prod of expectations, your own and other people's.

Look at Laura. Look what she had to do for her handmade rugs and her signed lithographs. Her career was an endless drill of in-cadence exercises, one two three four, and she couldn't see it wasn't worth it. Maybe do it for your flag, but not for your *things*.

He closed his eyes tightly, trying to block tears. Laura. No, he wasn't going to get sentimental about a woman who'd kenneled him.

Oh, this was an expensive kennel, to be sure—private room, garnished food, designer paper on the damned walls. The place probably had a classy name, too, Green Oaks or something. Laura always threw plenty of money at her problems.

With her Mercedes and her closets full of suits—completely seduced by the trappings. Didn't she realize it wasn't important what the curtains here looked like, or whether there were flowers at the communal dinner ta-

ble? Didn't she realize the place was no different in its
essence, in its function, from the damn veterans hospital?

Like the doctors at the vets hospital—like every
doctor he'd ever met—Laura had given up on him.

Well, fuck her. Fuck her. He'd been on his own before and he could do it again. And this time he wasn't
going to wait for a bunch of heel draggers to give him
their blessing. They told him sixteen years ago he'd need
"substantial assistance" his whole life. But the minute
they handed him his duffel bag, his walking papers, and
(like it was some big honor) his Purple Heart, he'd
struck out on his own. Completely on his own, except
for a month in jail. And three years with Laura.

He forced himself to sit up. His stomach was jumpy
and his head ached. He felt dehydrated and disoriented
in the dark room. The door was where, exactly? He
stood shakily and began feeling his way around the
room, his left hand skirting the cool papered wall. In a
couple of hours the nurse would bring in a wheelchair.
The nurses discouraged walking unless it was done in
the exercise room under their chipper supervision.
Laura probably approved; as a lawyer, she'd appreciate
their determination to avoid liability.

Suddenly his right leg gave out on him, but he caught
himself on the wainscoting, his heart pounding as he
imagined the racket he might have made. He massaged
the leg briefly, reassured to feel hard, well-defined mus-
cle there. His body was in good shape, all right. The
problem was his brain. It wasn't sending the right signals.

The trick of it, he remembered from the vets hospital
days, was to move what you could and pray for momentum.

Chew off your paw and limp out of the trap.

He edged closer to the door, using a Formica night-stand for support. A lot of concentration to do what once was automatic.

He looked out into the corridor. His head ached, and the left side of his forehead was so tender it felt burnt. He'd been wheelchaired up and down this hallway a dozen times. Why the hell couldn't he remember which direction to go? At one end, a glimpse of decorator couches. At the other, wheelchairs collapsed in an interlocking row, like supermarket carts. Nothing looked familiar.

He chose to go left, past the wheelchairs. His left hand gripped his right leg, dragging it like a weight strapped to his hip.

Turning the corner, he nearly collided with a young bearded man. The man blinked at him, obviously surprised. Hal stood there, feeling his heart race, feeling sweat collect in the small of his back and drip down to his waistband.

He tried to remember who the man was. Someone he knew from the common room? Maybe even his doctor?

His seventh or eighth month in the vets hospital, he'd had an encounter like this one, a middle-of-the-night showdown with a man in a white smock. It had ended with Hal's being forcibly returned to his bed, cast into the limbo of sedation. Then a month of Thorazine to "improve" his attitude. It was like being smothered, constantly, slowly smothered.

Now the bearded man said something to him. It sounded Japanese. Hal had heard a lot of Japanese when he'd done the gruntwork for a landscaper. But he supposed the man was speaking English.

Hoping for the best, Hal smiled and said, "Yes, that's right."

The man smiled back, then continued down the hall.

Hal could feel his right leg drag as he struggled down the brightly lighted corridor. He braced his shoulder against the posy-papered wall to take some of the weight off his hip.

Finally, he reached an open door. The physical-therapy room looked like a hoopless basketball court, with colored lines painted onto a shined wood floor, and mats stacked along the far wall. He'd watched patients shuffle across that floor, trying to keep within lines of a certain color. He'd walked the lines himself, his arm anchored heavily around somebody's shoulder. He'd lain on his back on a mat, trying to lift his leg, enduring the therapist's smarmy tape loop of encouragement.

Oh God, he thought, get me out of this place.

At the opposite end of the room, sliding glass doors led out to a small patio.

He ducked inside, panting now. He'd come too far to let them keep him in this hellish bit of cotton batting.

The room was empty, but so vast that Hal felt dizzy looking across it. He studied the floor like a map. The white line appeared to be the shortest route. He put his left foot on the line, and dragged his right. Without a wall to lean on, he felt suddenly vertiginous. He even considered, briefly, going down on hands and knees.

"Shit!" he heard himself hiss. He clamped his left hand to his right thigh again, reminding the thigh how to move.

Across the room, the glass doors framed a pale dawn. He could see a small cement patio circled by a short wall, and he moved toward it, trying to forget the process of walking, trying to walk as others walked, by rote. And his body finally got him there, though he'd veered far off the white line and onto a red one.

He rested his forehead on the glass door, heaving a sigh of thanksgiving. He happened to notice then that his pants were unzipped, but he left them that way, afraid to take the time to zip them, afraid he'd do something clumsy like smack the glass with his elbow.

He was relieved to feel the door slide open as he pushed it. He supposed the staff didn't worry about their slack-faced shufflers trying to escape.

The cold air felt good on his hot face. Later, he supposed, it would cool his sweat and make him miserable. But he'd survived winters of freezing rain in Washington and British Columbia. And from coast to coast, more times than he cared to remember, he'd awakened to night snow freezing his cheek to a sleeping bag. He'd be okay.

Judging from the scattered clusters of twiggy treetops beyond the cinderblock wall, the patio was surrounded by a newly landscaped parking lot. Hal stumbled past a rock garden full of bonzaied trees. He looked down at a stunted cypress, his chest tightening with horror. It was only a tree, not a symbol. But a panicked surge of adrenalin helped him pour himself over the wall. He landed hard on his shoulder and side, spitting out grit.

For a moment he sagged in the swirl of soot where the parking lot met the wall. There were only a few cars in the lot, clustered nearby. Beyond them, where the tarmac ended, a field sprawled gently uphill, gnarled with an occasional oak or clump of coyote brush. A decidedly un–San Franciscan landscape. Where the hell was he?

He began rubbing his forehead, as if to summon the

genie of a reply. Then he stopped abruptly, curling the hand and burying it between his thighs. He'd been a forehead rubber at the vets hospital. The head-injury ward had been a horror show of tics—jaw scratchers, nose tappers, earlobe pullers.

He stood shakily, noticing a red-brown stain on the arm of his fisherman sweater. He pulled up the sleeve. Blood was leaking from a saturated cotton ball taped to the inside of his elbow. He ripped it off. It made him feel marked; the patient's yellow star. It fell on a crushed 7-Eleven coffee cup and some dry oak leaves.

He looked around. The rehabilitation center was behind him, and the parking lot stretched in front for perhaps a hundred yards. At the other end was a long two-story building flanked by square signs, Red Cross symbols and ambulances. A hospital.

Immediately beside Hal, where the parking lot ended, were hills shagged with dried grasses. In the first light of morning they were the dull manila of paper bags.

He remembered driving down from the city with Laura once, passing countryside like this: low, thirsty hills dotted with oak and scrub. They'd come so Laura could shop.

His mind presented him with an image: the interior of a store, Laura handing a clerk her credit card. He could smell a hundred mingled perfumes and see a flash of sequins as the clerk bagged Laura's purchase. Whatever the thing in the bag had been, he remembered calling it a waste of good money. Laura had replied that good money is the kind cheap people spend. They'd eaten frozen yogurt in a ceramic-tiled courtyard that was supposed to fool hip patrons into thinking they were nowhere so déclassé as a shopping mall.

Yes, it made sense. City hospitals looked like hospitals. So Laura had taken him south (he remembered it was south), to the place where she bought her party dresses. She shopped at an ersatz park; she would kennel him at an ersatz bed-and-breakfast.

He moved toward the gravel verge between the tarmac and the grass, his left arm raised as if he were on a high wire.

He could brood later. Right now he had to get the hell away from here.

The grass was damply yielding, spattering fine night dew on his boots and the rolled cuffs of his jeans. It was more difficult to walk on the uneven ground, to coax the uncooperative leg uphill.

He tried to visualize a map, the map in Laura's car. It showed the curve of land around San Francisco Bay, and to the southwest, foothills colored yellow-green as they flattened into a dozen contiguous cities. There were no words (none that made sense to him) on Hal's mental projection, but his brain supplied a label: Stanford.

He stopped, out of breath, his heart pounding. Thank God. He knew where the hell he was. He'd fixed himself in space.

Stanford.

He recalled that it was fifty-some minutes south of the city by car. That meant six or seven hours by foot. If a man were well enough to walk it.

He was lurching downhill now, beyond the horizon visible from the parking lot. Almost out of sight. Close by, in a low-limbed live oak, a scrub jay tapped and jumped from roost to roost. If Hal could make it to the tree and sit awhile, he'd be okay.

He touched his forearm and felt blood still oozing from the pinprick on his inner elbow. His chest ached, and the muscles in his right leg (to the extent that he could feel them) were cramping in jerky spasms.

He sank to the ground, ten feet short of the tree.

He'd once known a direction-finding trick involving the sun's position in the sky. Right now, he couldn't quite get a handle on it.

He lay back in the grass, letting the leg muscles twitch. The rest of him felt limp, leaden. He stared up at wispy clouds and brightening sky. Sixteen fucking years. What the hell had set him back?

He'd been fighting with Laura, he remembered that. The same fight: her conspicuous consumption, her thoughtless waste, the way she relied on others—her housecleaner, her "personal shopper," her gardener, her caterer—to do her sweating for her. And the next thing he remembered he was alone on the carpet, half his body dead.

Oh Jesus. He and Laura had had an awful time. Fighting, stepping on each other. She called him cavalier, cynical, cruel. He didn't want to remember what he'd called her.

But this couldn't be her doing. Could it?

He twisted suddenly, regurgitating medication. He raised himself to hands and knees, shuddered with dry heaves.

It wouldn't be the first time a woman had fucked up his life.

He crawled a little closer to the oak tree, then he collapsed. His cheek scraped dry leaves and dart-sharp seeds of rye and fescue. The smell of damp ground filled his nostrils.

He'd awakened face down on the carpet. Alone. No matter how angry Laura might be, no matter what she might do in anger, she wouldn't leave him like that, would she? (But Jesus, he'd said some things to her.)

Hal squinted at the grass, rising in thousands of limply intersecting stalks. It was a surreal view; and a cold, paralyzing dread settled over him.

Maybe he wouldn't make it this time.

1

Dan Crosetti was trying to be smart, and his so-called friends were being bastards about it. Worse, I was supposed to be his lawyer, and I was a mess, running on automatic pilot and last-minute continuances.

I looked at Danny and felt guilty. Not that it helped him any.

He'd been to my office looking for me. But I'd walked out after starting my day in a showdown with Doron White, senior partner.

It wasn't easy for Crosetti to get around—a National Guard truck had taken off both his legs in 1972. Today, one of Crosetti's radical gofers had driven him to my apartment and helped him teeter up two flights of stairs on crutches and a prosthesis.

Crosetti's self-styled "comrade" now stood rigidly beside a bay window, hugging the crutches like Scrooge on Christmas morning. He stood as far from my Baluchistan carpet and down-filled chairs as he possibly could, scowling down at the eucalyptus trees and foggy lawns of the Presidio. The scruffy sliver of a man acted as if my extravagance might taint him.

Dan Crosetti sat in a giant cloud of a chair, his legs ending before the seat did. The artificial limb looked lumpy and overlong beside twenty inches of empty denim. With his barrel chest and bulging arms, his round face and full beard, he looked far too heavy to maneuver on a piece of molded steel and two wooden triangles.

Typically Crosetti, he rumbled, "Laura. You're not okay. What's wrong?"

As if he didn't have enough damn problems, that I should burden him with mine. It didn't take a hell of a lot to make me cry these days, but I wasn't going to cry on Danny's shoulder. Not Danny's.

"I'm sorry you had to come all the way across town. I thought I was going to be in the office all day. I—" I what? I haven't done a damn thing for you yet? "I'm really sorry."

He continued looking up at me, concern crinkling the leathery skin around his eyes. I wondered if he could smell last night's vodka, where it had eaten rings into the end table and dribbled onto the floor.

If he noticed, he showed no sign of it. Not like my banker clients, who'd have glanced pointedly at the two-finger run in my hose, at my untucked blouse, at the shoes I'd kicked across the floor, at hair that should have been labeled *sproing*! I looked as if I'd gone hand-to-hand with Doron White. Which would have been better than the politely seething "conference" that left my wings clipped to the skin.

Crosetti sat forward, his belly doubling over most of his remaining lap. His eyes were milk-chocolate brown,

warm with intelligence and empathy. "I thought something might be the matter. I thought we might need to
talk." He extended a hand. "I mean, we're friends first,
right?"

Friends. I turned away. Crosetti needed advice, he
needed a lawyer. He needed to think about himself and
quit showing solidarity.

"Do you want something to drink?"

"Anything." His voice was filled with concern.
"Whatever you're having."

I couldn't very well hand him a Stoli, not at ten in
the morning. But it would have been my first choice.

Goddamn hospital swore by its "limited visitation
policy"; it was hours yet before I could drive down to
see Hal.

I crossed quickly to the kitchen, trying to avoid the
mental picture: the resentful bewilderment in Hal's eyes,
the way he kept opening and closing his hand as if to
prove to me that he was whole and well.

Oh, Jesus.

I got out three mugs, carefully mismatched to mollify
Crosetti's comrade. If I'd had any with broken handles,
I'd have used them. I told myself it was for Crosetti's
benefit; he didn't need more grief from his "friends"
about me. But it was mostly guilt. Crosetti would have
found a more utilitarian use for his money than signed
mugs.

I filled the mugs with day-old coffee and microwaved
them. I wasn't up to grinding beans.

Crosetti took the coffee. The other man waved his
away, not deigning to look at me. I knew his rap on
me: That my use of trendy new defenses to acquit mass
murderers had discredited necessary and legitimate defenses; that I'd made it impossible for "politically cor-

rect'' lawyers to evolve appropriate defenses. It wasn't that different from Doron White's complaint, however much the two of them would hate having anything in common.

But I'd been honest with Crosetti about one thing. Two luridly publicized murder trials had created an association in the public mind: Laura Di Palma was the hired gun for guilty clients, not innocent ones. The antithesis of Perry Mason.

Crosetti had said, "Then we'll be good for each other."

And maybe we would have been, if I'd kept my act together. "I've been doing a shitty job for you, Danny."

Behind me, the comrade humphed. Crosetti stopped sipping the sour coffee.

"Are you okay?" Crosetti's voice, deep and troubled, twisted the knife of guilt. He cared about me. He'd trusted me with his freedom; and I hadn't even taken time to make fresh coffee.

"I'm okay. But another lawyer might—" I thought of the lawyer Crosetti would probably choose, a politics-first soapboxer. It would hurt, watching the case go wrong.

Making a political statement was fine if you were looking at two months, or even two years, for trespass or destruction of government property; in those cases, publicity was the whole point. But Crosetti was charged with murdering his right-hand man—a man who'd turned out to be an FBI agent.

Crosetti put the mug down on the end table. His mustache and beard came together in a grim line. "We've got time to figure things out."

I sank into the couch upon which I'd spent the last six nights. I'd permanently creased wrinkles into the plump cushions. I smoothed them, not sure which way to go with Crosetti. He didn't need my excuses; he didn't deserve my problems. It would be unprofessional, and it wouldn't do anybody any good. Especially not Hal—not as long as it cost fourteen hundred dollars a day to keep competent help around him.

Fish or cut bait.

I looked at Crosetti. Round and legless, he looked like some bearish Humpty Dumpty. All the king's horses and all the king's men: The federal government had commanded its trucks to roll over protestors' supine bodies, and federal courts had ruled that Crosetti (the only protestor to remain in the road) had assumed that risk.

In an era of guilt over the lack of fanfare for returning Vietnam War veterans, people had forgotten the atrocities. They had forgiven everything done in the name of "patriotism." Even soldiers of the "war at home" now rushed to distance themselves from their acts of conscience.

But Dan Crosetti would never appear on Barbara Walters' television show, stammering apologies for having tried to stop that war.

I glanced at Crosetti's comrade. Wouldn't my politics surprise him?

"One thing I have done, Danny. I've waived the speedy-trial date. There's no percentage in hurrying. The delay gives us a chance to find out what really happened."

Crosetti's elbows sank into the soft arms of the chair. His face flushed. "How long—?" He laced his fingers, and for a minute I thought he was going to pray. Instead, he rubbed his woolly chin over his entwined knuckles. "Is it going to be . . . a very long time?"

Fear shined through his veneer of calm. I'd gone to see him in the hospital before the operation to save his legs was deemed a failure. I'd heard the same tone then, when he asked his doctor if the circulation had improved.

Waiting would wear him down.

The stomach cramps started again. I'd practically begged the doctor to tell me Hal would be better by a certain date, that it wouldn't drag on beyond the limit of my endurance.

Crosetti closed his eyes. As if on cue, his comrade stepped forward, clammy with anger, gripping the crutches like a weapon.

"What gets me—" He breathed hoarsely, scowling at Crosetti. "Danny went to a shitload of trouble to keep from killing anyone when it was supposed to be his duty as a good American. I mean, they literally rolled the fucking war right over him, because he wouldn't pick up a gun! Now they're trying to make out that he'd shoot somebody because he was *annoyed*."

Crosetti squinted at his friend, tears leaking into his crow's feet. "I just want it over with."

"It's the fucking government that should be on trial here, not—!"

"Danny, look." I shifted on the couch, putting the comrade more or less out of my range of vision, and, with luck, out of the discussion. "In this case, the longer the delay, the better for you. I know it's hard to wait, but—" Trust me; even though I haven't spared you half a thought in six days. "I'll check with my detective this morning. What we need right now is more information."

Crosetti seemed to waver, his gaze flicking from me

to his comrade, who now leaned heavily on his mentor's crutches.

"There's been some discussion about me going underground." He scraped his hands over his eyes as if to clear his thoughts. Or maybe wipe tears he hoped I hadn't noticed.

"Underground? That's crazy. You don't have any reason to, not at this point." I glanced at the legless length of denim. He must realize how conspicuous he'd be, how easy to track down.

"What if it came to that?"

I wrapped my arms around my waist. An hour earlier, I'd scornfully assured Doron White that Crosetti would never leave us holding his bond; that Crosetti was a facer of consequences.

"I'd think it was a shitty idea."

For the first time, Crosetti looked around the high-ceilinged flat. "Let's just say I've seen the other side of the system. The side that does this"—he tapped his prosthesis—"and gets away with it."

"Danny—"

"That sends a federal agent to become the best friend you ever had, and then tries to say you—" His mouth twisted into a red rectangle.

I sank deeper into the cushions. I'd seen that side of the system, too. I saw it every time I visited Hal.

"Danny?" He was my last criminal client; Doron White had made that clear. He was also my first innocent client. The first who'd touched a raw nerve of conviction; who made me want to win for his sake rather than my own. "I'll get you through this. Just stick around; stick it out. Please."

Crosetti slumped, round-backed, shaking soundlessly.

I got up, starting toward him. But he waved me back. His eyes were tightly closed, streaming tears, but he kept his arm extended like a traffic cop's.

I preferred to do my crying alone, too. I left the room, wandering down the hall to the bedroom. The one place everything had been okay for me and Hal.

It could be three months, it could be two years. He could get back the full range of motion and response, or he could remain alexic, aphasic, partially paralyzed, disoriented, hostile, and depressed. Brain injuries are tricky, Ms. Di Palma. And there will always be an increased risk of stroke, seizure, and mental disorder. But let's just hope for the best.

I picked up the bedroom phone ("message center"— I could hear the scorn in Hal's voice when he referred to the cordless, call-recording, call-forwarding unit by its proper name). I turned my back on the bed. The bedclothes were still wildly disheveled, comforter trailing to the floor. Usually a heavy sleeper, I'd wakened in a sudden panic; dashed out to the living room, knowing in my gut something was wrong. And I'd found Hal dressed in sweater, jeans, and boots, dragging himself toward the partly open front door.

I took a few deep breaths, caught a glimpse of myself in the bedroom mirror. I looked better than usual, that was the killer: sloe-eyed and tousled like some damn Italian fashion model. I averted my eyes.

Seven days ago, the police had arrested Dan Crosetti for the murder of John Lefevre, and I'd assumed the week's worst problems would be tactical and evidential. I'd anticipated some friction from Doron White (but not his furious ultimatum). And I'd been a little afraid, as usual, that Hal might leave me.

Only a week ago.

I forced myself back to that time, back to my role as Crosetti's defender. My own problems would have to wait.

I hit two buttons on the message center, and let my phone automatically dial the right number.

2

Sander Arkelett sounded drowsy, his voice slow and muffled. "Laura. Sorry. Let me get back on my feet here."

"On your feet? What's going on?" I'd phoned him at his office, not at home.

A brief pause. "I had, uh, kind of a late night—nodded off, I guess. How's Hal doing?"

"Better, I guess. They made a big production of wheeling him to the therapy room and having him walk toward me." I'd had to turn away, overwhelmed by the humiliation on Hal's face. "I've got to get him out of there, Sandy."

Silence.

Then, "We've been through this, Laura. The medication."

"I could get a nurse to do that."

"And if, God forbid . . . ?"

23

Hal has another seizure or stroke or whatever the hell happened to him.

I pressed my fist into my belly. "That's not what I called about. Dan Crosetti's here. I need to know what you've found out."

"Well . . ."

A four-year association, intimately close before I found Hal, had taught me what "well . . ." meant. "He didn't do it, Sandy. I've known Danny a long time."

"Non sequitur. But I'm not saying he did it; I wouldn't know. I just know it looks like it. Number one: He bought himself a rifle. Why does a pacifist buy a rifle all of a sudden?"

"The gun seller identified Crosetti? Positively?" Last I heard, the pawnshop owner had been waffling—suffering the convenient amnesia of a merchant with a reputation for discretion.

"Yuh." A note of surprise. "Yesterday."

Information I should have shaken out of the police by now. I was a sorry excuse for a lawyer.

"Crosetti never mentioned . . ."

"You didn't *ask* him?" Sandy sounded incredulous.

"No. I just assumed—" I'd talked to Dan once in jail, but I'd been in a rush, on my way to court for a bank client. I'd arranged bail, waived the speedy-trial date, and then forgotten everything but Hal. "Oh God! Why would he buy a rifle?"

"Better ask him, sweetheart."

"What else do you have?"

"Lot of stuff about Lefevre. Born in Arkansas. Went to Ole Miss." He hesitated. "ROTC, Vietnam infantry 1968 until the big pullout, did his FBI training and then worked out of Providence, Rhode Island, and Boston,

Mass. Then he dropped undercover, and I draw a year and a half blank. FBI won't say what he was doing— classic Fibbie bullshit's all I get. Six months ago Lefevre took some kind of leave of absence—I'm working on that. And then a month ago he went back on the job and started cozying up to Crosetti." Sandy tsked. "All the organized crime in this country and the white shirts piss away a month on *pacifists*." His tone held little admiration for either group.

"What about the other people at the Clearinghouse? Lefevre was spying on them, too. Anybody with skeletons in the closet?" I could hear the two men in my living room. Crosetti's voice was low and sad, the other man's high-pitched and agitated.

"I got a list as long as the Bay Bridge. To my knowledge there's something like thirty fringe groups using Crosetti's storefront to coordinate their activities. You phone, and they answer 'Peace Clearinghouse.' You tell them which group you want and they take a message."

"I know." The Clearinghouse had been on the corner of Twenty-fourth and Diamond since before I'd moved to town in 1971. I'd done some staffing then; helped with the draft counseling. Mostly I'd used the Clearinghouse to crawl out from under a teenage marriage, to escape the bell-jar propriety of my hometown. "But it's got to have regulars. Places like that run on the energy of eight or ten people, tops."

"So you want the short list. Okay, I'm on it."

Any of Crosetti's committed co-workers would have been infuriated to learn about Lefevre; any of them would have considered it the most ghastly of betrayals. With luck, the short list would contain the name of Lefevre's murderer.

A tone sounded in my ear; another call coming in.
"Hold on, Sandy."

I switched to the incoming call. "Yes?"

A breathless voice quavered, "Ms. Di Palma?"

I felt a knot climb my windpipe. The stroke-center
receptionist, I was sure of it. "Yes."

"One moment. Dr. Spane would like to speak to
you." She clicked off.

I closed my eyes and pressed the receiver more firmly
to my ear. He couldn't be dead. Couldn't be.

In the living room, Crosetti's companion was shouting, "Should have known he was bullshitting!"

Crosetti's reply was quiet at first, rising to an agitated
". . . on *our* side, and I still believe it!"

"Ms. Di Palma. This is Dr. Spane. I have some dis-
turbing news, I'm afraid."

I sank onto the bed.

"Mr. Di Palma seems to have left the facility."

A euphemism? " 'Left'?"

"He appears to have changed into his street clothes
and gone out through the therapy room. We, uh, found
some evidence that he went over the wall—the low wall
around the garden—and um, we've been over the two
or three acres closest to the facility carefully but we
haven't managed to locate him."

I caught my breath. "You mean he *escaped*?"

"Well, not to quibble with your word choice, but
from whatever motivation, he seems to have removed
himself—"

I pushed the hang-up button, switching to my other
line. "Sandy. Are you still there?"

There was a clunking, as of a receiver being lifted
from a hard surface. "Yuh?"

"Sandy." I couldn't seem to breathe. "Hal's gone.

He escaped from that— Oh God, I knew he'd hate it, but they said the first two weeks are critical and that he needed— Sandy, what if he has some kind of attack out there?''

"Hey. If he got himself out of there, he's in better shape than they thought. He'll be okay till we find him.''

"Pick me up.''

"There in ten minutes.''

A twenty-minute crosstown trip. "Hurry.''

I stood with shaky haste, shedding my work clothes and pawing through drawers for jeans and a shirt. I wasted a lot of time getting them on; couldn't seem to do anything without wasted motion.

I was vaguely aware of Crosetti's voice raised in angry praise of loyalty; something about loyalty transcending its object in the same way that pacifism transcends specific wars.

By the time I left the jumbled mess of my bedroom, Crosetti's comrade had begun his shocked rebuttal.

"Shit, Danny—that's exactly what they said about Vietnam! 'My country, right or wrong!' We all thought—''

"I'm sorry," I interrupted. "I have to go. I have to take care of a family— Oh, no!'' I remembered an ex parte motion I was supposed to argue at four o'clock. No use adding malpractice to my problems.

I crossed to the living-room phone, and called my secretary. "Rose, I can't make my four-o'clock motion, but I need the ruling. Somebody's going to have to argue it for me. See if Jerry's free. Or Hannah. Give them the file—it's not that much material.''

"All right." I could hear the trepidation in her tone.

Doron White would explode if he learned she was shopping around my motion at the last minute.

I surprised us both. "*Fuck* Doron!"

I hung up, turning back to my guests. Dan Crosetti had tucked his crutches back under his arms, and was trying to straighten himself out of my down chair. The effort, or perhaps his argument with his companion, had left his face flushed.

He clumped awkwardly toward me, crutches sinking into the deep-piled area rug. "What's wrong, Laura?"

In the street, a car horn popped, three long, two short. Sandy.

I didn't meet Crosetti's eye. "I'll phone you later, Danny. I need to ask you some questions."

I grabbed my purse and ran downstairs.

3

"**D**ID I TELL you I knew Lefevre?"

The sun was sinking below a horizon of ragged hills. There was barely enough light to see where we were walking. Even Sandy, in his surefooted desert boots, had begun to tread cautiously. My leather flats were painted with dirt, my thin socks porcupined with burs.

It was getting cold, a sharp night chill replacing the flaccid heat of afternoon. I had no idea where we were, or where the hospital might be in relation to us. My head rang with the doctor's laundry list of what might happen to Hal if we didn't find him by nightfall. The worst would be a stroke. Or there might be drug complications: anticoagulants making him bleed too freely, antiseizure drugs reacting to beta carotene in food, heart medication sapping his energy and possibly triggering arrhythmia. But the drugs would have begun to wear off by now, and after listening to the range of side effects, I thought it might be just as well.

29

"Exposure." My voice sounded flat in the open air. No halls of justice from which to resound. "He didn't say it, but that's what the doctor's worried about. If Hal stays out here all night in the state he's in—" I stopped, hugging myself. Sandy's anorak had been around my shoulders for the last half hour, but it didn't make a difference. It was weariness that made me cold. And fear.

"Stop it." Sandy's voice was gentle. "If he's out here, we'll find him."

I heard myself cackle at the inanity of the remark. "Find him? We've been looking for over six hours."

Sandy, usually calm and level-headed, snapped, "Well, what in the name of Jesus do you suggest? We're doing what we can do."

I couldn't see him very well in the fading light, but I didn't need to. I'd seen him in tuxedos and in jeans; I'd seen him without either. I had him memorized: tall and thin, slight slouch, blondish hair combed off a broad forehead, narrow face, long dimples when he smiled, deep furrows when he frowned.

"Keep walking," he urged. "No use standing in the cold."

We had half an hour of dim light left. We'd taken a different route back, but we both knew we were done for the day. That we'd failed.

I hesitated, turning to survey the dark landscape. How could I leave Hal alone out here?

"Laura!" Sandy's voice was sharp. "Did you hear what I said?" His arm circled my shoulder and he began walking, forcing me to move with him. "I knew Lefevre."

The baked straw smell had cooled out of the air. The twitter of birds had given way to the scratchings and scamperings of night creatures. I let Sandy propel me, but his words didn't quite sift through my dread.

"Lefevre! Come on, Laura—let's talk business."

Business. How did he expect me to give a damn about—

"Dan Crosetti's supposed to be a friend of yours." His arm tightened around me. "Right?"

"Later."

"No. Now." There was conviction in his tone. "I knew Lefevre. Ask me how."

"Jesus, Sandy." I was in no mood to have questions pried out of me.

"Ole Miss. We went to college together."

We walked in silence for half a dozen steps. I wondered vaguely why he hadn't mentioned it before.

"Lefevre was an odd one, Laura. Not to look at, or anything. He looked like a pretty regular guy."

It was beginning to sink in. "You knew the FBI agent. The guy who got killed." I shook off his arm. "Why didn't you tell me before?"

"This is the first time we've talked more than two minutes about the case, that's why." His voice was carefully nonjudgmental. "I didn't know him very well—wasn't sure it was the same guy till I got confirmation from Ole Miss."

"What do you mean he was an odd one?"

"This is second-hand. I called a friend of mine this morning used to room with Lefevre. He says every time something happened that Lefevre didn't like, minor stuff that happens to college students—run-in with an asshole professor, hassle with the registration people, putdown by some girl, whatever—Lefevre would be up all night typing."

Typing. Some news. "So what?"

"Whatever happened to him, he'd type into a transcript. But fictionalized. Happening to a guy who always thought of the perfect clever thing to say, who made the other guy look like an asshole. In the transcript, Lefevre called himself Jones."

We walked in silence for a while. The ground had lost its distinguishing features. It was uniformly dark, with enough holes and rocks to make it dangerous to the careless ankle.

The small part of my mind that could be spared from fearing the worst about Hal digested what Sandy had told me about Lefevre. An insecure, seething college student who'd found solace in fictionally demolishing anyone who insulted him.

"Jones," I mused. "Cool and in charge, like an FBI agent."

"Like what they think they are, maybe."

"Yeah?"

"Assholes!" Heartfelt loathing that surprised me, considering Sandy'd been a cop once himself. "When I was on the force, they'd breeze in looking for information and they didn't give a shit what kind of operation we had going or how long we'd been working on it. They'd blow our operation and burn out our informants to get what they wanted. They'd take credit for our work, and move on." It had been fifteen years since Sandy had left police work, but he still sounded bitter. "Demigods," he concluded. "You'll never hear a good word about 'em from a cop."

"Jones." In the back of my mind, a tune was spinning. "There's a Bob Dylan song about a Mr. Jones. Bizarre things are happening all around him, but he's not hip enough to know what they mean."

Sandy snorted. "Bob Dylan? I can't see a future Fibbie getting into that kind of shit."

I supposed joining the police force in 1968 (after two years in the army), had been Sander Arkelett's reaction to that kind of counterculture "shit." "Maybe Lefevre chose the name as a reaction against the song."

"Show he was a strait-laced guy? Could be."

We'd come to the top of a hill. Surprisingly close, the parking lot of the stroke center flickered with orange-tinged lamps, just coming on. The building itself was brightly lighted, inside and out; a beacon for the policemen, interns, and aides searching for Hal.

I stood at the crest, looking down. Returning might mean good news: that Hal has been discovered and consigned to bed. (Would Hal consider it good news?)

Or it might confirm my worst fear.

I turned to Sandy and let him pull me into his arms.

"They didn't find him." Sandy's words rumbled in his chest. "I arranged a signal."

I tried to ask him what kind of signal, but Sandy kept me pressed tightly to his chest. Somewhere, beneath a thin layer of broadcloth, he sported the scars of two bullets he'd taken working for me. He'd spent eight months recovering from them.

"Laura, I know you. You'll hate yourself if you let the Crosetti case get away from you. You've got to split part of yourself off from this thing with Hal. You've got to have a little faith—"

"Faith!" I struggled to push him away.

"Faith in Hal. He got himself out of a situation that didn't suit him. He may be sick, but he's smart. He took care of himself for a lot of years when he was probably worse off than he is now. And anyway"— Sandy let me push him away—"what's your alternative?

Curl up and have a breakdown? That won't help Hal, and it sure as hell won't help Dan Crosetti.''

He was a dark figure against a purple-gray sky. Behind him, the last sliver of sun scrolled behind the horizon.

It was on the tip of my tongue to accuse Sandy of hating Hal. No secret that he found Hal acidic beyond endurance, that he resented losing me to a man who didn't treat me like a lady.

"Look," he begged. "I'm not saying forget about Hal. I'm just saying don't let yourself fall apart. Other people need you. Crosetti needs you.''

I walked quickly downhill, hoping Sandy was wrong about the signal.

4

"**Y**OU ARE OBSTRUCTING justice," I repeated.

There were two of them, a dark-haired, low-browed one in a brown suit and white shirt, and a tall, suave blond with practiced dimples. The lowbrow sat at a steel desk, files tidily (and discreetly) tucked label-edge under a blotter. He was flanked by flags, framed by a gaudy government seal. The other man was perched on a corner of the desk, looking down his nose at me.

He turned on the dimples. "That's certainly not our intention." A bemused glance at his partner. "But you know we can't release classified information."

"You most certainly can. What you can't do is withhold information necessary to the defense of a capital crime."

We listened to the sigh of air-conditioning.

Finally Lowbrow sneered, "I don't see any subpoenas."

I suppressed a surge of fury. It was the standard gov-

35

ernment game: the FBI wouldn't tell me what kind of documentation, if any, existed. Then it dared me to subpoena documents I couldn't name or describe.

"My client is innocent. That means someone murdered an FBI agent and got away with it. You should jump at the chance to cooperate with me. I just need to know what Lefevre was doing—"

"Classified," Dimples repeated. Then wearily, "I don't know how many times you need to hear it."

"I need to hear a reason why I should take your word for it."

Every vestige of dimple vanished. "What's that supposed to mean?"

"You've offered no legal authority for withholding information to which I'm entitled under the Fourth and Fifth Amendments. I question your motives."

The other man laughed. "You're barking up the wrong tree, there. We didn't even know Lefevre."

Dimples cast him an annoyed glance. I may not have shaken much out of "the white shirts," but at least I'd gotten something. Lefevre had been dispatched from another city.

I remembered what Sandy had told me about Lefevre working out of various New England cities, and I took a guess. "Oh, we'll be talking to your Boston office, don't worry."

"Do that." Dimples looked smug. I'd guessed wrong. "But I suggest you leave the insinuations at home."

I'd seen myself criticized in a dozen national magazines and twice that many newspapers. I'd listened to state assembly floor debates outlawing a defense I'd pioneered. Every polite synonym for bitch had been used to describe me. Some impolite ones, too. I'd been smacked in the jaw in the heat of a deposition. I'd been threatened with lawsuits—one by the widow of a U.S. Senator.

I was too tough to be affected by snide posturing.

But I dashed out of that office. I hurried through the Federal Building corridor, crying.

I felt fragile. I hated it. It scared me.

5

I HUNG UP my office phone after smoldering through another lengthy apologia: The doctor had done everything he could be expected to do, from prescribing the right medication to ordering the proper therapy; he couldn't be expected to patrol the hallways himself, could he? He blamed his underlings, he blamed the physical layout of the facility, he even blamed Hal. I distilled my fury into a single sentence, striking where I saw an exposed nerve: *You'll be hearing from my attorney.*

Hal had been missing for thirty hours now. I was reasonably sure he hadn't collapsed in the hills surrounding the facility; the police had been searching since sunup. Either Hal had walked fast and far, or he'd hitchhiked out of the immediate area.

Sandy called it good news: Hal was well enough to elude searchers, well enough to put some miles between himself and the hospital.

Good news? Jesus.

If Hal was well enough to do that, he was well enough to call me. I had to face it: he hadn't just escaped from the hospital; he'd escaped from me.

Before he moved in with me, I'd seen Hal twice in thirteen years, both times by accident.

I ran into him in Golden Gate Park in 1981. I hadn't seen him since December of 1970, when he'd rolled out of our hometown in a bus full of draftees. He'd left behind a mother stonefaced with fury that he'd refused to avoid the draft by attending Princeton. His father (my papa's second cousin) had taken refuge in a bottle of Johnny Walker Red, knowing, while his big-shot friends applauded Hal's patriotism, that his son had boarded the bus to escape the family's string-pulling affluence.

That day in Golden Gate Park, I almost hadn't recognized the boy with whom I'd endured a thousand family dinners, the boy with whom I had nothing in common but relatives. It took me a minute to see behind the scowl and the stubble, the deeply creased cheeks and the salt-and-pepper hair. Hal had waited a long time to lose his patina of popularity, his rich-boy ease, but he'd done it with a vengeance.

We'd had a ten-minute conversation, Hal shading his eyes and looking away whenever I mentioned the family. I gave him my address and he pointed to a rusty van.

It was two years before I saw him again. Three years after that before we reconnected.

If he followed that pattern now . . .

I vacillated between fear and anger, never sure which emotion was more appropriate or more endurable. I'd spent most of the night driving around Palo Alto and most of the morning crying. I felt like I had a head full of cotton and an anvil on each shoulder.

But the bottom line was I'd hate myself if I let Dan Crosetti's case go to hell. Danny deserved better.

I assigned two law clerks to find out how to force information out of the FBI. I assigned a third to work on the appealability of convictions arguably resulting from information withheld; with incentive, the district attorney might join me in applying pressure.

I had had my session with the FBI agents.

I had threatened Hal's doctor.

When Doron White strode furiously into my office, I didn't care. Why not continue yesterday's showdown? My mood could hardly get worse.

White looked at my stark white walls and my bright, nonrepresentational collages. He looked at my silver-gray carpet, my red leather chairs, my table-sized desk with its Deco details. As usual, he shook his head slightly. His office looked like a box of men's stationery.

Always stately, Doron had become quite trim since his heart attack. He had the face of an aging thespian and hair to match, a wavy spectrum of grays parted to emphasize a dramatic streak of white. His dress was nautical, blue blazer and sharply creased gray slacks; on him, not at all informal.

I was surprised by a tug of nostalgia: he'd been so proud of me, once. Proud of my skill in winning acquittal for a man who'd shot two senators in front of hundreds of witnesses. White had started out as a criminal lawyer before deciding that (as he put it) it was better to pay the bills.

We watched one another warily. Our last conversation had degenerated into a shouting match.

"Laura."

"Doron." I waved him into my only non-upholstered chair, a masterpiece of zigzagged hardwood.

He sat on the very edge, neatly crossing his legs. "San Francisco's a small town," he said.

I stopped breathing. Had he learned about Hal?

"There's a rumor circulating that you screen cases based on ideological considerations." His tone bristled with affront.

"What do you mean?"

"You acquitted a man who killed two United States Senators because they were hawkish about the war in Vietnam. Now you're representing someone who has made a career of anti-establishment lawbreaking." He leaned forward with a pinched scowl. "Bluntly, people are wondering if you are expressing your own political ideology."

"If I'm a commie?" I tried to keep my tone even. "Dan Crosetti is innocent. It's not a question of ideology—mine or his."

Yesterday it had been finances: the firm was gaining a reputation for its (my) criminal defense work, and potential commercial clients were not considering us when they selected outside counsel. Worse, the firm was suffering from negative publicity, a law-and-order backlash that blamed the firm for the sins of its clients. And considering my significant pro bono donation of billable hours, White concluded, he had no fiscal alternative but to screen my cases before allowing me to accept them.

He thought he could treat me like a teenager asking for the car keys—in spite of the fact that I was the firm's top-billing associate, slaving nights and weekends to offset my pro bono work. In spite of the fact that I'd

put Doron White's one-in-a-thousand little law firm on
the map.

The hell he'd screen my cases!

"Let me put it another way, Laura. After our discussion yesterday, I assumed you planned to withdraw as
Crosetti's counsel. Today I learn you have three clerks
working on the matter."

"If I left the impression yesterday that I intended to
withdraw from this case, I apologize. I agreed to represent Dan Crosetti, and I intend to honor the commitment."

"Yes," he said dryly, "to the detriment of your other
commitments. Like yesterday's Waterford Bank motion."

"That was a family emergency. Unrelated to the Crosetti case."

I saw White glance at a snapshot in my bookcase:
Hal, with his characteristic scowl. White had only met
him once. A whim had brought Hal to last year's firm
Christmas party, where he'd spent the evening in silent
rigidity, drinking vodka and aborting every effort to en-
gage him in small talk. It didn't take much to get past
Hal's snide unsociability—a little warmth, a little hon-
esty. Not the bulldozer confidence of a Doron White.

"Well, Laura, whatever the reason for the last-minute
botching of that motion—I assume you know Jerry came
back with an unfavorable ruling?—the issue remains:
What do you plan to do about the Crosetti case?"

"Win it."

White slipped his hand into his pocket. I could hear
the click of heart pills in their plastic container. I wondered if it was conscious or unconscious, White's rat-
tling of nitroglycerin pills whenever anyone upset him.
He might as well brandish a vial of the stuff.

To my surprise, White pulled the amber cylinder of pills from his pocket. My phone buzzed with an incoming call, but White said, "No! Let Rose take a message. I've given this"—he held up the cylinder—"a lot of thought. It has changed every single aspect of my life. In every respect, personal and professional, I am semi-retired." He frowned, looking inward. I'd have frowned, too, if I'd been forced to spend more time with White's drawling princess of a wife. "I suppose you know to what I attribute the attack."

I glanced at my message light. If White planned to blame me for his heart attack, I wouldn't put up with it. He had nothing but his own irritable perfectionism to blame.

"We touched on the firm's financial problems yesterday," White continued. "Now you're telling me that, in spite of my frank explanation, you remain committed to what may well become another year-long battle."

"If my billable hours decline, complain to me then. They didn't slip during the law-school-murders case, did they? At least, not below the associate average."

"This is your sixth year with us, Laura; you are under consideration for partnership. We expect a great deal more from you than the associate average!"

"And you get more. Month after month." I started out of my chair, then forced myself back down. "I think that entitles me to *at least* the customary degree of autonomy enjoyed by other associates."

I wanted to say more, but I forced myself to shut up, take a breath, wait. No use forcing Doron to fire me. It had been a long haul getting through college and law school, getting the legal experience I needed to interest a blue-chip firm like White, Sayres. I liked my job—

and right now I had eighteen thousand dollars' worth of medical bills.

The ball was in White's court.

His lips were pinched into a tight white line and his cheeks showed unhealthy spots of color. "Tell me honestly: what are you trying to accomplish here?"

"I'm trying to help an innocent man."

"And it's just—what?" His lips twisted into a sneer. "Coincidence? Happenstance that he's part of a political movement whose ends you've previously served?"

Who the hell had White been talking to, anyway? "I proved that Wallace Bean was insane, Doron—insane to assassinate senators because of their politics. Anyone who thinks I sanctioned his actions is an idiot! And as for my politics—" Part of me rebelled against answering so intrusive a question. Then there was the part of me with bills to pay. "You've known me long enough to judge for yourself whether I'm some kind of subversive."

We stared at one another, strangers after a six-year association. I tried to remember the bit of labor law I'd learned in law school. I'd taken Crosetti's case before White issued his ultimatum. Could White make the ultimatum retroactive? Fire me for refusing to withdraw?

I guessed White wasn't sure. He stared out the windows beside my desk, hoary brows puckered into a frown. I waited a minute or two, knowing I should say something else in my own defense.

Instead, I picked up my receiver and pressed the message button.

My secretary greeted me with the cheerful statement, "That was Hal on the phone."

I held my breath, turning my chair away from White. "What did he say?"

She giggled. "You'll want to call him back on this one, Laura. He said it was about last week. He said, 'I was going after Dan Crosetti that night. I don't remember why.' " She read the message in a flat singsong, adding, "He said to tell you he thought it might be important." Again she giggled.

I didn't care about the message. "Did he say where he was?"

"No."

"That he'd call back?"

"No. He said not to bother you, just to tell you."

Not to *bother* me? Jesus Christ. "Local call?"

My secretary sounded surprised. "I didn't ask."

"That's all he said? Every word?"

"Well—he said hello and stuff."

"What stuff?" I could hear White tap the hardwood chair arm impatiently.

"You know. I asked how he was and stuff."

She'd been taking phone messages from Hal for three years. And Hal had a decidedly more pleasant manner toward the clerical staff than toward the attorneys. "Did he say how he was?"

"He said he was getting by, or something like that. Something polite. Is—? Should I have come in and gotten you, or something?"

"He didn't say he'd call back?"

"No."

"Call my house. If you reach him, transfer the call to me immediately."

I hung up reluctantly. No use asking her the same questions over and over, but I wanted to; nothing else seemed even remotely important.

I turned back to White. He was flushed. Angry with me for conducting personal business in his presence.

I didn't care. Hal was alive somewhere.

I prayed for the buzz of a transferred call.

White rose. "Well, Laura, I'm sorry we've come to this pass." He breathed audibly, quick breaths through flared nostrils. "I think there's something to be said for going by the book in a situation like this. I've given you my opinion and you've given me yours. I think the next step is for me to discuss the matter with the other partners."

I squinted at my wall clock, jotting down the time. The phone company would have a record of long-distance calls the firm had received. Sandy could trace the calls taken in the last ten minutes. One of the numbers might lead to Hal. If not, we'd know he was in the city.

I nodded to White, not quite sure what he'd said. Then I picked up the phone and pushed the message button again.

"No answer at your house, Laura."

Without replying, I hung up and dialed Sandy. I got his answering machine first, then his answering service. He was still out searching for Hal.

I slammed the phone down in frustration, then looked up to find Doron White watching from the door.

He gripped the heart medication, his fist slightly raised. I was startled by the sparkling fury in his eyes. He'd been so careful to control his temper—at least on the surface—since the heart attack.

I stood up, expecting the tidal wave of wrath that used to flow frequently from the otherwise dignified man.

But White turned away, slamming the door behind him.

6

I HAD NO idea where Hal was and no idea how to find him. I could only focus on his message. I flattened the message slip on my blotter, staring at Rose's dull, perfect cursive: *Last week. Was going after Dan Crosetti that night. Don't remember why.* (Thinks might have been important.)

The boxes labeled *Will Call Back* and *Please Return Call* were unchecked.

Last week. I'd been absorbed with Crosetti most of the day before Hal collapsed. I'd arranged an expedited bail hearing on the ground that Crosetti's disability required immediate and specialized medical attention. The hearing had gone well. Crosetti was a good risk; he'd been arrested several times without ever jumping bail. Besides, the judge had chastened the district attorney, how easy would it be for a paraplegic to skip town?

By early evening, I'd gotten Crosetti out of jail, using

the firm's money to purchase the bond. A violation, it turned out, of a canon of ethics stating that lawyers may not advance their clients the costs of litigation. But even if I'd remembered the canon, I'd have violated it without scruple: it was clearly designed to protect the lawyer, not the client. And for that very reason, I later learned, Doron White regarded it as holy scripture.

I'd been up against a tight deadline in a bank matter, so I'd left Crosetti with his usual comrade, assuming we'd talk in the morning. I'd gone back to my office and worked like a fiend preparing a writ of possession that had to be served first thing the next morning. I'd dragged my weary bones home at around eleven.

I remembered my fight with Hal in painful detail. It had hardly been out of my mind for six days; I'd reviewed every word, every nuance of it, asking myself if some gesture, some accommodation might have defused it. Asking myself, in a hundred indirect ways, if I'd triggered Hal's stroke. (A stroke being the doctor's best guess, "based on symptoms; since the preexisting brain damage makes CT scan images murky and uninformative.")

I shied away from the memory. Too much of what Hal had said was true. And too little of it was amenable to change.

I forced my focus to narrow: Had I mentioned Dan Crosetti?

I must have; I'd lived and breathed Crosetti most of that day. I'd have mentioned the case sometime before or during the argument; at least mentioned bailing my old friend out of jail. But what else had I said? What would make Hal want to go out later that night looking for him?

I was startled by the buzz of my telephone. I'd instructed Rose to hold all calls except from Hal, Sandy, or the Woodside Stroke Center.

I pounced on the phone. "Hello?"

"Sandy." He sounded a little out of breath. "What's up?"

"Hal called."

"What'd he say?"

"I didn't talk to him." He could have gotten through, damn him. "He left a message."

"What did he say?" A frantic undercurrent. For hours he'd been driving back roads to cafés, gas stations, anyplace Hal might have stumbled into.

I blinked tears out of my eyes; tried to keep them out of my voice. I read the four terse sentences.

"That's it?"

"That's it."

"Didn't say where he is?"

"No."

"Get me permission to access the firm's phone records?"

I hesitated. "I haven't told anyone here about Hal."

A short silence. But no "why not?" Two gory murder cases had made me the object of as much gossip and speculation as I could handle. My co-workers didn't need to hear about this.

"Okay, I'll get on it. Probably just as fast to do it my way. But Laura . . . ?"

I knew what he was wondering. Why would Hal have set out after Crosetti in the predawn hours? "I don't know, Sandy."

"Did he know Crosetti?"

"He never said so. He must have heard of him back in the seventies." There had been months of debate about Dan Crosetti: Had he assumed the risk of being run down? Did he have it coming for refusing to move? Did the government have the right to ignore standard procedures for removing protestors? To risk the life and limb of civilians?

"Did you talk to Hal about the case?"

"Probably. At least in passing."

Sandy tsked. "If he had something to tell Crosetti—something about the case—why not just tell *you*?"

Because we'd stopped speaking at around one-thirty that morning.

"We're missing a connection here," Sandy concluded.

7

I PULLED MY Mercedes into a loading zone two and a half blocks from Crosetti's Clearinghouse for Peace—a good parking place by San Francisco standards—and walked up Twenty-fourth Street. The Noe Valley had once been an area of three-family Victorians and unsophisticated neighborhood shops. It had been comfortably working class, far enough from centers of commerce and tourism to be allowed its unmemorable shabbiness. But in the last half-dozen years the exquisite taste of young professionals had transformed it like a Midas touch. The neighborhood was now spruced-up and chic, as befitted the entrance to the dazzling bustle of Castro Street, the "gay capital of the world." But Diamond Street was far enough from Castro to have retained some of its old plainness. It had been scraped and painted, but not (yet) over-ornamented.

The Clearinghouse itself was a drab rectangle with faded matchstick blinds and windows plastered with an-

nouncements: caravans to Washington to lobby for
AIDS research and health-care funding; local rallies to
end hunger, to end the war in Central America, to end
the arms race; hunger strikes, walks, and demonstra-
tions to show solidarity with farm workers, Palestin-
ians, and Salvadorans; performances to benefit the
AIDS project, battered women, the homeless, the disabled, and the Socialist Workers party. There were announcements of petitions within: in favor of the
domestic-partners ordinance, rent control, disarma-
ment, and the release of Russian prisoners of conscience; opposed to workfare, mandatory blood tests,
aid to the Contras, and the roundup of illegal aliens.
Glancing at the jumble of beseeching messages, I felt
tired. Sucked dry by measured phrases to judges and to
bankers and to the senior partner of White, Sayres &
Speck.

I walked into a room of tattered easy chairs, stacks
of *Mother Jones* and mimeographed tracts, thumb-
tacked posters and a wall-sized photomural of the AIDS
quilt. A dog lolled on a braided rug so dingy it was
impossible to guess its original colors.

The room had a different feel than it had had in 1971.
It was less crowded, less psychedelic, less charged with
the anger of war resistance. But something about it—
the smell of dirty floor and dusty paper, maybe—stirred
a few ghosts: my determination to break free of a suf-
focatingly strict upbringing and an unfaithful husband,
to express myself any way I could—politically, intellec-
tually, sexually.

Like me, the Clearinghouse had become more busi-
nesslike. Beside the door were four telephones on two
multi-drawered, old-fashioned desks. A woman sat at
each desk. One of them was slumped into an armadillo

ball of arms wrapped around knees. A telephone cord disappeared into a cascade of brown hair. A voice from the center of the ball said, "It's a media creation. Junk. You can't take it seriously."

The other woman sat very straight in new denim and a starched pink shirt. She spoke into a shoulder-trapped receiver. "You might look up the article he wrote for *Peace Train* in 1983." She watched me come in. "That will explain his objectives in some detail. Lend texture to your profile."

Fifteen feet beyond the desks, behind the arrangement of sagging easy chairs and pamphlet-strewn end tables, behind a wall of acronym-labeled filing boxes and a twitching mound of sleeping dog, stood two men and a woman.

One of the three was Crosetti's "comrade," the one who'd visited my apartment the previous morning. He didn't seem particularly glad to see me. He motioned the woman, fiftyish with severely chopped gray hair, to be quiet. I moved forward quickly enough to hear her say, "Danny knew him better than we did!"

I stepped around the shoulder-high stack of boxes. "Have you heard from a man named Hal Di Palma?"

"Ask Sara or Barbara." The comrade waved toward the phones. "They've been taking the calls."

I looked back at the two women. They were still glued to their receivers.

A skeletal young man with baggy clothes and a shy smile stepped forward. "You're Laura Di Palma, aren't you? My crim.-law professor thought you were great." He blushed.

A few theoreticians admired my success with long-shot defenses. Everyone else filtered my performance through some moral stance.

The severe-looking woman edged closer, frowning into my eyes with (I thought) studied forthrightness. "You're Danny's lawyer, aren't you? Can you tell us what the fuck is going on?" She stumbled a little over the profanity. A fifties housewife, clawing her way out of the cocoon?

I glanced again at the woman on the phone. Still engrossed in conversation. I definitely had a little time to kill. And these people were, after all, part of what Sandy called the short list.

"I'd rather hear your thoughts." I looked from her to the comrade to the law student. "Anything you can tell me about John Lefevre."

The comrade snorted. "You'd think we each knew someone different!" He scowled at the gray-haired woman.

She raised her arms and let them fall in a pantomime of exasperation. "As well as we know Danny, to be so quick to discount his opinion! He knew John the best. All we have is the government's word for it that he was an FBI agent."

"He was an FBI agent." I pricked her bubble of blind faith. "Working out of a New England office, I think."

"New England?" Her eyelids fluttered in surprise. "He told us—"

"That's the whole point!" Crosetti's comrade was livid with anger. "Lefevre lied to us about everything. I can't *believe* we're standing here wondering if he was a nice guy at heart."

The law student interjected, "That's not what we're saying. This is about Crosetti, not Lefevre." He frowned. "Lonita's just saying Danny knew him a lot better than we did."

The older woman—Lonita, I assumed—nodded vigorously. "They ate together, they swapped manuscripts. They practically lived together. Danny's take on Lefevre is certainly as valuable as yours, Keith."

"Crap! If that was true, we wouldn't have had a federal agent in our bosom for the last month."

I found myself agreeing with Comrade Keith.

"You said they swapped manuscripts. Do you have any examples of Lefevre's writing?" I asked Lonita.

"Danny probably does. They used to critique each other's work."

I tried not to get my hopes up. If Lefevre had continued his "Mr. Jones" transcripts, I might be able to learn who had been angering (and maybe been angered by) him lately. I turned back to Keith.

"You disliked Lefevre all along? Even before you learned he was an FBI agent?"

He took a backward step. "Not enough to kill him!"

Touchy, touchy. "I wasn't implying anything. From what I've heard, Lefevre was smart and likable. If you had a different impression, I'd like to hear about it."

Behind me, a female voice: "*I* had a different impression."

The straight-spined woman had left her post by the telephone. She extended a manicured hand, saying, "Barbara Nottata." She did it in a practiced way that suggested much contact with the public.

Our handshakes were equally firm; no wimps here. "I'm Dan Crosetti's lawyer."

"Laura Di Palma. You've been in the news often enough for me to know that."

The wrong button to punch. "You didn't like John Lefevre?"

She shook her head. Her hair, moussed into a modern

female version of Fabian's, didn't move at all. Surrounded by grimy rugs and thumbtack-riddled walls, she had a level of grooming that seemed extraordinary; what I might find in a lawyer's office.

"I can't really point to any one thing," she mused. "And of course now that I know he was a spy, I'm sure I saw signs of it in everything he did."

The older woman made a snorting sound. "I don't think any of us had ten minutes to spend on personal chitchat with him. It troubles me that we're willing to conform our beliefs to what we've been told is true. Danny says even if Lefevre did come here to spy, he'd become one of us; that he would have quit the FBI and joined us."

"That's egotism." Keith dismissed his mentor's theory. "Sure, Danny's preaching is persuasive—to us. But we're the proverbial 'converted.' "

"He's persuasive to a lot of other people," the law student said reasonably. "Nonconverted people."

"Well, here's what I thought I noticed." The well-groomed Barbara took back the reins of conversation. "Each of us has a particular focus."

Keith shook his head sourly. "Support groups!"

She didn't blink an eye. "Mine happens to be rape crisis counseling and child-sexual-abuse support. And not"—she returned the sour look—"the more general goal of ending world hunger. But what struck me was John's interest in abuse issues when he talked to me and his equal interest in Soviet Jewry when he talked to Lonita."

Lonita eyed her with obvious disapproval. "Most of us don't limit ourselves to a single issue. We have a broader agenda."

"Also"—a crease marred Barbara Nottata's smooth

forehead—"did you ever say anything teasing to him? Or watch him when he got a crank phone call?" She looked intently at the others. "He'd get this pinched-up look."

The law student said, "It's pretty hard to draw conclusions from a 'pinched-up look.' "

How judicious. "What was *your* impression of Lefevre?"

"I don't know. I mean, he seemed like what he said he was. But obviously he wasn't."

I turned back to Barbara Nottata. "Did you get a call from Hal Di Palma today? For Dan Crosetti?"

She shook her head. "*I* didn't." Then she rapped her knuckles on one of the cardboard boxes stacked beside us. "These are our mailboxes right here, if you want to check."

For the first time, I noticed that the back side of each box, the side where I now stood, had a labeled manila envelope securely taped to it.

"Can you show me Dan's box?"

Lonita seemed on the verge of protesting, her lips pursed and her head shaking. But Barbara Nottata tapped a polished nail against a waist-level box.

Its envelope was empty.

"Danny was here a couple of hours ago," Lonita volunteered. She seemed to take satisfaction in adding, "He took his mail when he left."

Barbara frowned at the box. "We've had calls for him since then. I've taken several."

"Can I see the messages?"

She shrugged. "Sure."

She led me to the desk occupied by the young woman hiding behind her own hair. The woman was saying, "About half of them are in jail for the rest of the day.

The others are camped on the tracks waiting for the afternoon munitions train, but it'll be there any minute. I can get you tomorrow's site information, if you want. Also Nuclear Watch spotted one of the new H-bomb trucks on 580 near the Broadway exit. They need some people to track it.''

Barbara Nottata reached past her, picking up a sheaf of messages and depositing them on the other desk. She made a "Help yourself" gesture.

I sat at the desk. It was stacked with fliers and petitions and alternative newspapers. There was a row of messages torn off a three-by-five white tablet, with hasty initials in the top left corner indicating the intended recipient. The tallest stack bore the initials DC.

One of the phones rang, and she reached past me to pick it up. I noticed a dainty wristwatch and a silver bracelet. She stood behind me, murmuring, "Hello," and then, "Yes, go ahead."

I sorted quickly through two hours' worth of Crosetti's messages. There was one from a professor wanting to reprint an article of Danny's in an anthology. One from his doctor, about coming in again to get "measured." The rest were from reporters or well-wishers. I noticed that the desk was checkered with sheets marked DC but bearing only the first word or two of a message. Barbara obviously saw no point in memorializing hate calls.

Behind me, she was counseling her caller to remain AWOL until he received some legal advice.

It startled me. Despite obvious differences in mood and emphasis since 1971, the Clearinghouse had, in this respect, remained the same. What I had done years ago, and Barbara did today, someone else would do years from now: there would always be a scared kid out there, going AWOL.

I made two piles of Danny's messages, pushing aside those from reporters. I reread the others. *Our love and support, Your friends at Glide. Remember what Gandhi said—"First they ignore you, then they laugh, then they crack down, then you win." Love, Daniel and Philip. You don't know me, but what you did changed my life— Good luck to you, teacher.* There were half a dozen more in this vein. I read them several times, but only one of them had the slightest potential for containing a hidden (or confused) message from Hal. It read: *I remember you from the hospital. I know it wasn't you.*

Hal didn't talk much about his war injury. Had he and Crosetti been at the same hospital sometime?

I put the message back on the stack, discouraged to find myself clutching at so slender a straw. Crosetti had been in and out of hospitals since 1972. He'd met and inspired a lot of people there.

The long-haired woman beside me was talking about where the "site people" would be tomorrow. Barbara was flipping through a directory of attorneys, the telephone receiver still wedged against her shoulder. At the other end of the room, the law student crouched beside the dog, scratching its ears. Keith and Lonita sat on doghair-covered easy chairs, going over a list together. I saw no sign of grief or sympathy for Lefevre. Apparently only Dan Crosetti cared about the murdered man.

It jangled some subliminal nerve; left me feeling something was missing from the picture.

I considered asking Keith or Barbara for names and addresses of other regulars, but decided I'd leave compilation of the short list to Sandy.

There was a chance in hell Hal had called Crosetti

this morning; a chance in hell Crosetti had taken home his message. Maybe even a chance Hal had remembered his errand and gone to see Crosetti at home.

I'd have visited Danny anyway. We needed to talk about the rifle. We needed to talk about Lefevre.

But it wasn't professionalism that made me dash to Crosetti's apartment.

8

I SURVEYED THE dreary neighborhood that had once served a thriving shipyard, slaughterhouse, ball park, and racecourse. Thousands of blacks, fleeing economic devastation in the South, had settled into rickety temporary housing that managed to outlast every industry it was designed to support. In a city of shared walls and fresh paint and hilly vistas, Hunters Point had a flat, worn homogeneity, an atmosphere of nothing happening and every kind of mischief brewing.

I knocked on Dan Crosetti's door, one of the few in the city that was flush with the sidewalk. The building might have been a small warehouse at one time, a plain three-story box shadowing tired double-deckers. It was close enough to the old shipyard to reek of rusting metal and polluted bay.

I'd never been to Crosetti's apartment before. I'd known from the address that it was in Hunters Point, but I'd let myself suppose it was in some gentrified, or at least hip, enclave. Now I doubted such an enclave existed. The Chamber of Commerce happily factored Hunters Point into its average cost of city rentals; otherwise, it might as well have been on Mars.

It came down to money. The government had cut off Danny's disability checks, listing a variety of "sedentary" jobs he was capable of performing. I'd seen the list in a *Mother Jones* article. It had been compiled by a bureaucrat flipping through a government catalog of jobs, jobs like cranberry sorter and condenser aligner. Not one of the listed jobs existed in San Francisco; and even if they had, Danny would have been competing with most of Hunters Point for them. A Social Security Administration shill had suggested Crosetti move to an area of "greater economic opportunity." Never mind that moving would eat up several months' worth of checks; never mind that Crosetti might not be hired when he got there. The SSA had its orders: deny all claims.

A group of tall black teenagers rounded a corner. Seven or eight of them, athletically dressed. Probably more blacks than inhabited the entire county I'd grown up in.

I told myself I wouldn't react with a knee jerk of fear; I was more acclimated and more enlightened than that. On the other hand, Crosetti's front windows were barred, and I could see weathered scars of a crowbar around the lock of his front door.

I knocked again, feeling a little sick. The most dangerous things about my neighborhood were falling eucalyptus branches and the occasional rogue golf ball from the Presidio course.

As the group came closer, I tried the doorknob. I

told myself it was to save Danny the trouble of hoisting himself onto his crutches.

The door was unlocked. I swung it open and slipped inside, slamming it behind me. I heard the teenagers laugh as they passed the barred windows.

"Danny? It's Laura."

I looked around the living room. It was a clone of the Clearinghouse: old braided rug, third-hand chairs, mountains of papers and notebooks and clipped-out articles. The difference was, here everything was pushed back, leaving the center of the room open for maneuvering. The walls were covered with old political posters ("Who Owns the Park?"), Xeroxed calendars of events, and Nuclear Watch route maps.

"Danny?"

I could hear a television set on the floor above; a game show, inane and raucous. I could hear shouting down the street, someone telling the teenagers to wait up. As I walked across the living room, I heard something else. It was the faint, quiet lapping of water.

"Dan? Are you in the bath? It's Laura."

The lapping of water continued, accompanied, I thought, by a wistful hiss of breath.

Five steps had taken me across the living room and onto the grimy planking of a hallway. There was a small kitchen on my left, with a table but no chair. There was a bedroom straight ahead with an unmade bed and a long, cluttered desk. To my right was a wheelchair that looked small for Crosetti. I'd seen him crammed into it once or twice, but he seemed to prefer crutches.

And I could see why. The wheelchair, however narrow relative to Crosetti's girth, could not possibly have squeezed through what I guessed was the bathroom door. However much of a physical strain the crutches might be, and however uncomfortable the prosthesis, at least Danny could get himself upstairs and through doorways with them. At least he could look people in the eye.

The bathroom door was ajar. I tapped on it. "Danny?"

Again the wistful exhalation.

I hesitated. I could hardly walk in; Danny had so much to keep private. But I wished he'd make up his mind to answer me. "Danny!"

His voice drifted through the small opening, weak and slow. "Don't come in."

"Are you okay?"

"Sure."

I put a hand on the doorknob. "Do you need help?"

"No. I'm all right. But you don't want to see this."

"You didn't answer. Your door was unlocked." I frowned at the chipped porcelain doorknob. The smell of mildewed tile and old plumbing wafted through the door. "Are you sure you're okay?"

"Yes." He sounded far away, drifting. In the tub, eyes closed, deep in a trough of misery; that was my guess.

"What's wrong, Danny?"

A splash, a soft laugh. "What I did."

What he did. My hand dropped from the knob. I wanted Dan Crosetti to be innocent. He had to be, for both our sakes. "You mean buying a rifle?"

"Yes."

"Why did you buy it?"

"Pissed." His breathing was labored and audible, except when footsteps pounded over the floor upstairs. "I thought they'd fucked me every way they possibly could. My legs, my court case, my piddly-ass disability check. You know how many times I've been in jail now, Laura?'' There was a clipped tightness in his voice. ''Know how many times I've heard the joke about the inmates' baseball team needing a new third base? Jesus, they love that one.''

''Danny, come out, okay? I don't want to talk to you through a door.''

''I liked John. I liked him just about as much as I ever liked anyone in my whole life.''

''Why?''

''Because,'' another splash, ''because he came across like such a fucking grouch. But he really wasn't.''

I thought of Hal, rebuffing conversation at the law-firm Christmas party. That's what always got me— knowing what the mordancy masked.

As if reading my mind, Crosetti said, ''Did Hal tell you?''

''Tell me what?'' My voice was sharp. ''Have you seen Hal?''

''The night I came by.''

''What night?'' My arm twitched to throw open the door.

''That first night. Poor John.'' A faint keening filled the air. I wasn't sure at first if it was Crosetti.

''Danny! What night?''

The keening grew louder. Definitely Crosetti. I stood in the dark hallway in a sweat of impatience, wishing that he'd pull himself together.

''Danny, it's important! Please!''

The sound stopped. I waited; what else could I do?

''Danny?''

''What a disgrace. Not just for me, but for the whole Clearinghouse. Buying a gun like some kind of Rambo.

After everything I've been through. Everything I've said.''

"When did you meet Hal?"

"What did I lie in front of that truck for? To turn my back on everything and go buy a gun?"

"Danny—you didn't use the rifle?"

"I wanted to blow his head right off his body. Like we used to fantasize about draft boards. Like John was just some piece of government property." A choke of pain. "I threw it in the bay. Made me feel dirty, just having it here."

"When did you see Hal?"

"Hal? Oh. Middle of the night. I came to tell you. I didn't want to admit it when we talked before. And definitely not in front of Keith. God."

"So you—"

I was startled by a swooshing of water and a sound so shockingly guttural it hardly seemed human.

"Danny?" I considered flinging open the door, but presented myself with a quick list of reasons why I shouldn't: his privacy, my embarrassment, and (though I hated to admit it) a horror of seeing what his trouser legs concealed. "Dan!"

The swooshing subsided. The guttural sound stopped. All I heard was water dripping.

I stepped through the door preparing to apologize, to avert my eyes.

It was worse than I could have imagined. The damaged stumps of his legs broke the surface of the water like knobby, twisted islands. His scarred, bloated belly rose like another part of the archipelago. And the water—Jesus Christ.

The water was red.

Dan Crosetti had slid into a tubful of crimsoned water, his face fully covered, long wisps of his hair floating on the surface like jaunty flags. The back of one hand rested on the chipped enamel rim, with streaks of red flowing from wrist to forearm.

I took an involuntary step backward, my stomach lurching. My God, I'd been standing on the other side of the door while he bled to death.

I didn't think I could make myself cross to the tub.

He may not be dead. He'll drown if you don't help him.

It was only three steps, but I took the last two on my knees.

My hands were poised over the water. I had to turn my face, to focus on a peeling sliver of wall paint, before I could plunge them in.

My fingers encountered slick skin and I jerked back involuntarily. My silk sleeves splashed red water, drank it like a sponge.

I could smell urine and feces, part of the miasma. I'd smelled it in the hallway, attributing it to the plumbing. But it had been Danny, already letting go.

I slipped a hand under his head and brought it out of the water. His forehead came first, hair slicked against it, then his eyes, nose, mustache and beard, tainted water sheeting off.

"Danny," I choked. "Breathe!"

He began to slide, his head sinking. I linked my other hand behind his neck, pulling him back up.

I thought I saw his eyelids twitch, a bristling of his thick brows.

I fought a spasm of nausea; tried not to focus on the metallic smell I knew must be blood.

Danny's eyes opened. He looked calm, almost beatific.

I fought to keep his head above water, moving with him as his body continued its undignified slide.

His lips moved. *Let go,* he mouthed.

I couldn't pull him out; he was too heavy. Dead weight. And I couldn't leave to call an ambulance because he'd slip back under the water.

I groped in the tub until I found the plug. I pulled it.

For the long minute it took for the tub to drain, Danny watched me. At first, his face was flaccidly empty of expression. Then his chocolate-brown eyes winced in comprehension. He moaned, "Oh no."

I left him like some overturned beetle in a shallow stream of fouled water. I staggered out of the room, dripping from both sleeves and heaving.

I could have let my friend die a dignified death, but I didn't.

9

I STUFFED MY clothes into a garbage sack. I never wanted to see them again.

I had padded Danny in blankets, slipped pillows beneath his head and dried his face until the skin began to slough. But nothing would remove the earlier image from my mind. I'd never forget the position in which I'd left him when I went to phone an ambulance.

I'd let his life blood drain away while I stood politely on the other side of the door, ignoring the weakness of his voice and the pain of his litany. I'd changed the subject, over and over, asking him about Hal.

And then I'd robbed him of a quiet suicide. I'd interjected flashing ambulances and panting men and nurses with forms to be filled out.

Dan Crosetti had wanted to die at home, to slip peacefully out of his life. Instead, he'd died after much noise and jostling, with tubes in his arms and needles stitching the slashes in his wrists.

69

God.

I stood under a hot shower until the water started to cool, something I couldn't remember happening before in my nice, modern apartment.

It was six-fifteen by my bedroom clock. Almost five and a half hours since I'd walked into Danny's. Three hours since Danny had been pronounced dead. An hour since I'd finished talking to several nurses, a doctor, a uniformed policeman, two plainclothes detectives, and the assistant district attorney prosecuting the Lefevre case, in that order.

And I had a lot of talking left to do.

Phone calls to Crosetti's friends.

More important, phone calls to reporters. No fucking way I'd let the police and the DA close the Lefevre case.

Dan Crosetti had not killed John Lefevre; and however much the jocks up in Homicide wanted the FBI out of their hair, I wasn't going to let them stamp the case "closed," not yet.

Nor was I going to let Crosetti's political enemies label him the "pacifist-murderer." If I could prevent it, no one was going to be as unfair to Danny as he'd been to himself.

Crosetti had been angry enough to buy a rifle, yes—but he would never have used it. Lefevre's murderer had robbed him of that essential piece of knowledge. Lefevre's murderer had yanked out moral underpinnings that were more important to Danny than his legs had ever been.

As far as I was concerned, the FBI and Lefevre's killer had conspired together to kill my friend.

I didn't care if the FBI padlocked its files and wrapped me in chains: I would find out why they'd assigned Lefevre to the Clearinghouse. I would find out why the United States government wouldn't leave Crosetti alone, after all it had done to him.

I would do that tomorrow. Tomorrow was for Danny. Tonight I couldn't get past wanting Hal.

10

ANOTHER DAY I'D have prepared carefully for a press conference. I'd have chosen the appropriate suit, depending upon whether I wished to project strength, optimism, or right-headedness. I'd have planned and rehearsed my statement with the same deliberation I brought to jury trials. But then another day my desk wouldn't have been stacked with things that should have been done last week. The love of my life wouldn't be missing, crippled and disoriented somewhere. I wouldn't have discovered my client—my friend—in a tubful of his own blood.

I sat at my desk, watching the sky over Telegraph Hill lighten, my desk lamp spotlighting the mountain of papers between me and malpractice. Doron White would have a fit when members of the press began filing into the firm's conference room, when inelegant technicians began setting up lights and taping electrical cord to the carpet.

White would have heard about Crosetti's death by now. Was he breathing a sigh of relief? Glad his august and conservative law firm had avoided the stigma of defending a pacifist?

He'd have a few things to say about the press conference, all right. He'd shake his bottle of heart pills like some pinstriped rattlesnake. But I had yet to be forbidden—by official vote of the entire partnership, anyway—to continue representing Crosetti. White could hardly fire me for doing what I was still entitled to do.

It might be impolitic of me in the year of my partnership vote to press the issue, but I had little choice. The dignified paneling of our conference room, the gold-leaf FIAT JUSTICIA on the podium, the sheen of the walnut tabletop—they would lend weight and authority to my words. They would tell the journalists and their television audience that I was no crank—no mere pacifist—to be dismissed out of hand.

White, Sayres & Speck, willing or not, would lend me the credibility I needed to thumb my nose at the police, the district attorney, and the Federal Bureau of Investigation.

I hit the button to activate my speaker phone, then punched in Sandy's home number. I'd waited as long as I could stand to wait.

Sandy answered, sounding groggy.

"Sandy, where have you been? I tried until almost three in the morning to reach you."

"Laura. Jeez, it can't be much later than that now."

"Six-thirty. Did you find out anything?"

"Hal's in the city, or at least he was when he made that phone call." He yawned loudly. "You have any idea how many calls your firm gets? It was a chore and a half just checking on the long distance.'' Another yawn. "Sorry, sweetheart. You say six-thirty?''

"In the city." Thank God. "He must have hitched a ride. If you could find out who picked him up, we'd at least know where he was dropped off.''

A short silence. "Look, if Hal's getting around okay, making calls . . .''

"What's your point?''

"If he wanted you to find him, he'd have told you— I guess I don't like the idea of looking for someone who doesn't want to be found.''

"You didn't see him in the stroke center, Sandy. We're not talking about someone who's getting over the flu. He's got serious problems! He could—''

"Hey, hey—don't get upset. You know I wouldn't let you down. I'm just saying he might not thank you.''

I closed my eyes tightly. Hal might be too confused or sick to come home. He might be too resentful to want to. Either way, I couldn't stand to think about it. "Did you hear about Danny?''

"Crosetti? No. I sort of put that one on the back burner. What's up?''

"You don't know? You didn't hear the news?'' I opened my eyes, forced myself to sit up straight. I'd be telling the story to the press in just two hours. I had to be able to talk about it.

"Come on, sweetheart. What's up?''

"I went to his apartment yesterday at around noon. His door was open and I walked in. He was in the bathtub, so I stood on the other side of the . . .'' I took a few deep breaths. God, I should have rehearsed. I'd have to do a lot better for the cameras. "I talked to him through the bathroom door. He said he— he was depressed. Because he'd bought a rifle.''

"Did he confess? Did he say—"

"No. He didn't use it. He threw it in the bay."

A brief silence. "Why'd he buy it?"

I tried to explain Crosetti's anger—his fury that the government had taken everything he had and still wouldn't leave him alone.

"The government harassed him literally to death, Sandy. He'd cut his wrists. He was bleeding to death in the bath the whole time I talked to him."

"Oh, Jesus! Sweetheart—you all right?"

"No."

For a while, neither of us spoke. I tilted my chair and squinted out the window at the bright white sky. A trick of the hills perched tiny Victorians on the shoulders of financial-district monoliths.

Finally Sandy spoke. "Definitely suicide?"

"No possible doubt. I pulled him . . ."

Grimly, "Go on."

"I pulled his face out of the water when he slid under. He told me to let go. And when he, um, when I let the water out of the tub and he knew I was going to call an ambulance, he said, 'Oh no.' "

"You see the razor or knife or whatever in the tub?"

"God, Sandy! I wasn't exactly looking for it."

"I'm sorry, really. But— look, I know you weren't paying conscious attention to the little stuff. But just think back, okay? You walked into the bathroom, and you saw—"

"Oh my God."

"What?"

"I walked into the bathroom and I saw Danny. That's all." I pressed my hands against my eyes. "Except for the fixtures, that's all."

"No razor? It might have been underneath him—"

"No crutches. No prosthesis. Sandy, his wheelchair was out in the hall—it was too wide to fit through the door. I assumed Danny got out of it on the crutches."

"Except there weren't any crutches by the tub."

"No."

"Well. That's a wrinkle."

I felt limp in my chair. My eyes itched from lack of sleep, my shoulders ached with tension. "I can't— I just don't get it." But I had to get it—before the press conference, in fact. The police had certainly noticed what I, in my trauma, had not. And by now a few enterprising reporters had the information, too. "Sandy, what does it mean?"

"It means someone carried Crosetti in, or carried the crutches out." He sighed. "But that's not what you're asking, is it? You're asking who. Why."

"A friend."

"Yuh. I can't see Crosetti letting a stranger put him bare-ass in the tub."

"But a friend wouldn't hand Danny a razor blade."

"Well, it could be the other way round. Crosetti gets himself in there on his crutches. Gets out his razor. Lowers himself to the rim of the tub, puts aside his crutches, runs the water, takes off the false leg, gets in."

"And someone comes in later and takes the crutches and leg away?"

"So Crosetti can't change his mind."

"Maybe he just—could Danny have crawled to the tub?" I wished I hadn't said it. I'd hated to think of him scraping his torso over that dirty plank floor.

"Why would he?"

I tried to keep my breathing steady; didn't want Sandy to know I was crying.

"Well," he mused, "it's your call: Do we concentrate on finding Hal, or figure out what happened with Crosetti?"

What a choice. I pushed the disconnect button.

11

H<small>E WAS PROBABLY</small> the stupidest judge ever to hear a law and motion calendar. I couldn't rely on my responsive papers. Even if the judge had read them (which I doubted), he'd obviously missed the fine points of law with which I'd demolished my opponent's argument. I tried now to explain my position in the simplest possible terms. But like many judges, this one was infuriated by anything that contradicted his misunderstanding of fact or law.

I would leave the hearing with financially disastrous news for my bank client. Its regional vice president had a history of making bad loans, and would try to cover his incompetence by blaming me. Under ordinary circumstances, Doron White would have backed me up. But after this morning's press conference, I'd have a hell of a time convincing White I hadn't given the motion short shrift.

The judge concluded, ''I am persuaded that the relief

from stay requested by Borstmann Properties is under these circumstances both appropriate and warranted.''

And I'm a purple cow.

I was in no mood to return to my office. White was probably still in a fury—he'd actually put one of the nitroglycerin pills under his tongue this morning.

I stood listlessly in the cavernous lobby of City Hall, checking my calendar. A tide of city workers surged around me. A couple of them I knew, but I wasn't up to small talk and they left me alone when they saw I couldn't summon the requisite smile of greeting. Here and there, tourists stood like cargo-laden islands, focusing cameras at the building's intricately carved and gilded dome.

A man stepped up beside me. I noticed the suit, bland and inexpensive. I wouldn't have looked at his face if he hadn't spoken.

"Here for the press conference?"

His tone was snide. The FBI agent who'd warned me to stop making insinuations, the one with the killer dimples.

No dimples this morning. He looked like a poker player trying not to let a great hand show.

He couldn't mean *my* press conference. What the hell was going on? "Are you?"

He nodded.

The FBI wasn't big on press conferences, and when they did have them, they invariably chose their own Federal Building digs. The DA and the Homicide Detail usually chose the Hall of Justice, where they and their staffs were quartered. "Why City Hall? Neutral territory?"

The FBI agent shrugged. "Not at all. Our investigations have been fully cooperative and parallel in nature. No jurisdictional problem."

Right.

"Show?" The Hall of Justice was a drab structure full of pinchpenny furniture. A press conference at City Hall meant stock news footage of a colonnaded exterior, of vast marble staircases and a dome to shame cathedrals. Maybe the government needed its stage setting as much as I'd needed mine.

Dimples dropped behind me as we climbed the curved stair. He probably kept his back to the wall, too.

When we reached the second-floor landing, I was careful to let him lead. The opulent disutility of the lobby meant a rabbit warren of tiny offices upstairs. I wasn't sure I could find the pressroom.

The agent led me to a small room that stank of stale cigarettes and vending-machine coffee. He entered, but I hung back, looking through the open door. Glass-walled cubicles along one wall displayed messy desks and equally untidy reporters. In the middle of the room, a dozen journalists fiddled with tape recorders, fanned themselves with notebooks, chatted, laughed, gulped coffee. On either side of them, TV reporters angled for unobstructed views of the room's only table, which had been pushed to the far end of the room. They leaned against walls or squatted on one knee or propped their elbows on the table, balancing minicameras on their shoulders. Each had a dressed-up partner, kibitzing and conferring and directing. At the back of the room, technicians angled lights on rickety metal braces and taped electrical wire to the floors.

At the only table, a deputy district attorney sat like a dour movie star behind a bouquet of microphones. Her lacquered hair and aquiline nose made her look like a helmeted warrior surveying the hordes. On her left sat a balding old walrus from Homicide.

I watched the FBI agent thread his way through the crowd to the far end of the room. He leaned across the table, murmuring something to the deputy DA. She looked up sharply, scanning the audience.

It's bad form to crash the opposition's press conference. If the reporters noticed me, they'd begin filming my reactions, trying to goad me into public confrontation. If I could avoid that, I would. But damned if I'd leave just because it was seemly. I wanted to hear what the government had to say, and I didn't want to settle for the bare-bones media version.

The deputy DA rapped her knuckles on the tabletop. "Ladies and gentlemen." Like a faint chorus of crickets, cameras began to whir. "As you know, I am Melissa Pran, deputy district attorney for the city and county of San Francisco. On my left is Inspector Daniel Krisbaum of the San Francisco Police Department, Homicide Detail." She looked around the room as if daring someone to disagree with her. She overdid the hostility in the courtroom, too, often creating juror sympathy for the accused. "At this time, we would like to issue a joint statement regarding the disposition of our investigation into the murder of John Jules Lefevre."

Inspector Krisbaum muttered something to her. She nodded.

"As you know, on the tenth day of this month, the state arrested Daniel Morelli Crosetti for the murder of John Lefevre."

The reporters stirred, wanting news, not preliminaries.

"As you also know, Daniel Crosetti died yesterday

afternoon at four-forty-eight P.M.'' She tapped a file. ''The death certificate issued by a medical examiner in the coroner's offices states that Mr. Crosetti died from loss of blood caused by three self-inflicted razor slashes on each wrist. After close consultation with the San Francisco Police Department and the Federal Bureau of Investigation, the district attorney's office has concluded that no further action by our office regarding the murder of John Lefevre is necessary or advisable, given the state of the evidence at this time.'' Her face puckered like a wilted apple. ''Questions?''

Loud, simultaneous questions from television reporters needing footage: ''Are you saying Crosetti killed himself because he killed Lefevre?'' ''Did Crosetti confess?'' ''Did Crosetti leave a suicide note?'' ''Is there evidence against anybody other than Crosetti?''

''Let me put it this way.'' The deputy DA made a point of looking judicious. ''At this time, the district attorney's office lacks sufficient evidence to bring charges against any other person. In consultation with the appropriate entities, we have decided it is appropriate to label the case 'active-inactive,' meaning that we would certainly reopen our investigation if new evidence came to light, but that unless and until that occurs, no further action is contemplated. Next.''

A woman with a notebook started to speak, but was elbowed aside by a woman from Channel 5. ''You've stopped investigating?''

''Again: unless and until new evidence is uncovered by the Homicide Detail or the Federal Bureau of Investigation.''

A jumble of questions filled the air, mostly for the Homicide inspector and mostly from television reporters.

The inspector rubbed his ear thoughtfully, apparently

trying to distill a single question from the din. "Unless we actually get a conviction in a case"—he waited for the room to quiet—"we don't technically close a file. But, uh, we also have an 'active-inactive' designation. Which is where we've got this case right now."

"Will your investigation continue?"

"Actively?" another reporter added.

A third mentioned me. "Crosetti's lawyer says he was 'hounded to death'—that his suicide doesn't mean he was guilty."

"Yeah, yeah." Krisbaum nodded impatiently. "Crosetti's lawyer! All I can say is, we were prepared to prove that Daniel Crosetti purchased a weapon of the type that killed John Lefevre—"

"Did you ever find the murder weapon?"

"No, we did not."

An explosion of questions, with Krisbaum shouting over them, "There are literally hundreds of types of gunpowder, and traces of a relatively unusual type were found on the victim's clothing surrounding the entry wound."

The reporters quieted down.

"There are fewer than a dozen establishments in this city that supply this type of powder, and the proprietor of one of them was prepared to testify that he sold Mr. Crosetti a hunting rifle and a small quantity of ammunition a matter of days before the crime took place. And no"—Krisbaum forestalled a question—"we did not find the rifle or the ammunition at Crosetti's apartment or anywhere else. And his attorney did not permit us to discuss the matter with him." A snide curl of the lips. "Or rather, Mr. Crosetti was advised of his right to remain silent, and he chose to exercise that right."

Danny hadn't needed me—or Krisbaum—to advise him of his rights.

"I think it's unfortunate Mr. Crosetti didn't have an opportunity to defend himself in court—" Krisbaum patted his glistening forehead with a handkerchief. Good; he'd look shifty on television. "But as to whether or not we continue investigating, we have to make a decision based on the evidence we have. Also we have to take into account the number of other investigations we have to conduct in the interest of public safety."

Shouted over quieter questions: "Do you have anyone actually working on the Lefevre case now?"

Krisbaum raised his arms in a small shrug. "I'm here, aren't I?"

The questions grew louder and more jumbled as mini-cameras prowled low around the table, seeking better angles. But the next ten minutes were more or less a rehash of the first two: As far as the authorities were concerned, Daniel Crosetti had killed John Lefevre, then killed himself. Further investigation would be a waste of limited law-enforcement resources.

From my obscure post by the door, I watched the dimpled FBI agent. He was leaning against a wall, arms folded. There was a look of malevolent satisfaction on his face, a suppressed peep of dimple, that kindled my frustration into a smolder of outrage.

I stepped out from behind the door frame, into the room. "Speaking of law-enforcement resources, why did the Federal Bureau of Investigation assign an undercover agent to spy on a legitimate, above-board, well-respected political organization?"

Reporters turned, looking uninterested until they realized who I was. Then a collective step was taken toward me. Telejournalists gestured frantically to their cameramen.

The deputy DA said coolly, "I am unable to answer any question relating to matters outside the scope of my office and expertise. I think that's all for today. I'll be available for standups."

But the reporters had lost interest in her, at least momentarily. I squinted into the dazzle of photographers' lights now turned on me.

Closing the investigation, with Crosetti forever labeled a murderer!

"If the FBI refuses to release the basis for and results of its month-long investigation, how can your office possibly determine who besides Dan Crosetti had a motive to commit this crime?"

Reporters were shouting to me. The question I heard over the rest was "Why did Crosetti do it?"

Jesus, hadn't they heard what I'd been saying? "He *didn't* do it! Dan Crosetti was a committed pacifist. Violence was absolutely against his principles."

Another din, another loud shout: "Then why did he buy a rifle?"

"Pain and frustration. But he did not use it! He threw it into the bay."

"Why did he kill himself if he didn't do it?"

I stared at the reporters, seeing Danny in a tub of red water. An Asian woman in a red suit bobbed suddenly through the phalanx, surging toward me. I stepped back, pinned against the wall.

The reporters shuffled a half step closer, breathlessly shouting variations of the same question: *Why did Crosetti kill himself? If he wasn't guilty, why did he open his veins?* The woman in red shook her head slowly, like an oracle.

If he wasn't guilty, why did he kill himself?

"Listen," I pleaded, "isn't it obvious? Can't you see why Dan Crosetti killed himself? He had nothing to live for. He was disabled and penniless, and he was facing the long ordeal of a criminal trial."

My voice was losing its modulation; I could hear the volume spiral. "After an arrest, I might add, based on virtually no evidence. While the FBI was burying the truth under Nixonian rhetoric, Dan Crosetti's reputation—practically the only thing he had left—was being destroyed. If Crosetti had gone to trial, the FBI would have been forced to stop obstructing justice. Now it's going to get away with withholding crucial information from the police and the district attorney."

The crowd became a blur. I could feel the sting of tears; feel myself shaking. "Based on this manipulation and misdirection, they're stamping the case closed—'active-inactive,' in newspeak—and the hell with Crosetti! The government didn't give a damn about Crosetti while he was alive, and it doesn't give a damn now. It doesn't give a damn about the First Amendment. It doesn't give a damn about civil rights or the disabled. It treats a Dan Crosetti like garbage and then pats itself on the back for forcing kids to say the flag salute."

Jesus Christ, I'd lost it.

I blinked the room back into focus. The reporters were staring in happy disbelief. I could almost hear them thinking: Great footage!

The deputy DA looked furious. The FBI agent grinned openly.

A roar of questions grew up in front of me, but I sidled to the door, striding quickly from the room. My outburst wouldn't help clear Danny's name. In fact, by tossing around accusations—attacking the *flag salute*, for Christsake!—I'd made myself—and by extension, Danny—look hotheaded and unpatriotic.

And it had happened in front of cameras. Damn.

12

Sᴀɴᴅʏ ᴡᴀs ᴡᴀɪᴛɪɴɢ for me at my apartment, pacing my living room in loose-limbed agitation. When he heard the door close behind me, he turned, starting toward me as if to say something. Then he stopped.

I must have looked startled; I'd forgotten he still had a key.

He gestured toward the door. "Didn't think you'd mind." But he looked a little wary.

"No." I bit my lip. "Did you find Hal?"

His lank hair fell over his forehead and he pushed it back with a long, impatient hand. "No." He bent from the waist, making himself nearer my height. His face was unusually flushed. "But, sweetheart, listen. You're going to like this."

I'd been fighting mortified tears for the last half hour, hoping to shed them in private. Whatever Sandy's news, I wished he'd phoned. I walked past him, kicking off my pumps and sinking into the couch.

He watched me, a frown flickering across his brow. "Lefevre's missing months—his six-month leave of absence—I know where he was."

"Lefevre?" I was distracted; couldn't seem to loosen the chokehold of my own humiliation. Not even for Danny's sake. "Where?"

Sandy sat beside me, slipping a wiry arm around me. "Right here in the city."

"Doing what?"

"Drugs. According to my source, a sixties-style headful. And listen to this: People in the neighborhood—Lefevre was living near the panhandle, off Haight—they knew him as John Jones. Mr. Jones!"

I stared at Sandy, catching the scent of his aftershave. There was a familiarity, a security, about sitting on the couch with him. As if I'd turned the clock back three years. In a way, I didn't want to hear about Lefevre. Didn't want to spoil the comfortable amnesia of the moment.

"Remember when we went to Big Sur to pick up Commerce Bank's collateral, Sandy? The two Lamborghinis?"

He was suddenly still. We'd taken a room together. I'd forgotten that.

"Mr. Jones," I repeated.

"Sounds like Lefevre—" Sandy's arm tightened around me. "Of course I remember Big Sur."

"The driftwood sculptures."

"Sure." A small smile curled his lips. "That's what it was."

"Sounds like Lefevre what?"

"Like Lefevre—" He shook his head as if to clear it. "Like he had a little bit of an identity crisis."

"Danny was sure Lefevre was sincere. He told them

at the Clearinghouse that even if Lefevre started out undercover, he ended up coming around to their way of thinking.''

"Well," Sandy was clearly troubled, "you know, I wouldn't necessarily interpret this Jones thing as the start of a political conversion. Not based on what Crosetti said, anyway. I mean, Crosetti would want to think so—wouldn't want to admit he was taken in. And Lefevre went back to Fibbie, don't forget."

"What's your theory?" It came out sounding like a challenge.

He scooted farther from me, his arm sliding from my shoulder. "I told you I knew Lefevre a little bit, long time ago. He was kind of weird then—this transcript thing he did. And being a white shirt wouldn't have made him any saner."

"You think he went slightly crazy."

Sandy slumped, rubbing the spot on his chest where he'd taken two bullets. "I do a little lying, a little undercover stuff in my job—have to get information somehow, right? And I'll tell you, it leaves traces." He blinked repeatedly, as if the thought were hard to face. "I mean, you tell yourself you believe in the system. But you cozy up to somebody, get him to trust you so he'll tell you stuff—personal stuff. Then you turn around and give it to some smart lawyer to crucify him with. I mean, fine—you do it for greater good and the integrity of the criminal-justice system. You help get information to those twelve good people on the jury, and let them decide, right? Except that deep down you feel like shit."

Though I'd never heard him express the sentiment before, it didn't surprise me. I'd seen his pinched frown when he handed me reports on witnesses I planned to "crucify." I'd glanced at him in court while demolishing a woman with information he'd tricked out of her friends.

"Speaking as the smart lawyer who 'crucifies' her witnesses—"

"I didn't mean this as an attack on you."

"I feel like shit sometimes, too. But it doesn't drive me off the deep end. That's what psychological defenses are for. And I'll bet Lefevre's were as strong as anybody else's." My voice sounded harsh, bitter. "Stronger, since he worked for the fucking government."

Sandy watched me, eyes narrowed.

"You'd rather believe Lefevre was crazy than believe Dan Crosetti converted him to pacifism."

"I'm not so sure there's a difference." He stood up, looking down at me, his face pale and glum. "Look, I've got a feeling this is getting personal, and I don't know why."

"You were a cop from 1968 to 1974."

"Yeah. So?"

I stood up, too. "Do you think the National Guard had a right to run over Crosetti?"

Sandy shook his head slowly—but not, I thought, in answer to my question. "You're using Crosetti as some kind of acid test. What the hell good is that going to do anybody?" He raised his hands, palms out. "I don't want to fight with you about stuff that doesn't matter."

"It matters to me!" The tears flooded out.

For a moment, Sandy just watched. Then he whispered, "Sweetheart? What's this about?"

I turned away. "Watch the six-o'clock news."

13

I LEFT THE television off, and I let my answering machine screen my calls (mostly from reporters; calls I'd never return). I dealt with my problems the same half-assed way I always do: I drank.

I meandered around my apartment, bottle in hand, casting a hostile eye on my showcase furniture, my sandstone sculptures, my lithographs and collages. My investment in the rug alone would have paid Crosetti's rent for two years. Throw in the end table, and he could have lived someplace nice.

I tried to congratulate myself for all the pro bono work I'd done, but that money had come out of the law firm's pocket, not mine.

I tried to feel entitled to my small luxuries. They represented the physical and emotional energy of six years' work (eight, if I counted my State Supreme Court clerkship and my year with the U.S. Attorney). I was productive with my

time—did I have to be productive with my lucre, too? I'd
given up a lot for it; wasn't it mine to squander?

But for the first time I understood why my cozy affluence offended Hal. He'd met too many Dan Crosettis
in his life.

Ironic to find a foothold of common ground now,
with Hal missing.

I sank into the couch, cradling my bottle of Stoli.

I might have been within ten feet of Hal tonight, shining
my high beams over the eerie foliage of Golden Gate Park.

Cruising the park had been a long shot anyway. There
were dozens of parks from one end of town to the other.
Golden Gate and Land's End alone concealed hundreds. That's what Sandy had said.

Mostly Sandy had ridden in sullen silence, determined to
protect me from lurking danger. *Bad detective work, a waste
of a night, a damn-fool idea;* he'd muttered many a testy
phrase. And he'd given me advice: "Look for him in the
daytime. Where he used to hang out in the daytime."

But frost tipped the grass of neighborhood parks, glinting
under streetlamps like sprinkled sugar. In every park, from
elegant Huntington to weedy McLaren, men and women
huddled on patches of dry dirt, layering themselves with
garbage bags and newspapers and old blankets.

"Sweetheart, you're just driving yourself crazy.
Chances are, Hal found himself shelter hours ago."

I'd seen Hal at the stroke center; Sandy hadn't. Two
days wasn't enough time to restore Hal's street smarts.
Not nearly enough time.

But I finally had to concede defeat. I was too tired
and too dazed to continue driving.

Sandy wanted to stay with me, but I said no. I was
sick of the voice of reason. Give me a bottle, any day.

14

I WOKE AT dawn, my stomach cramping, my first thought a familiar one: *You're becoming an alcoholic.* I hoped the fear would fade with my hangover.

In the meantime, Sandy had promised to continue searching for Hal. Small comfort.

And I needed to do something for Dan Crosetti; something requiring the authority of my profession.

I also needed to do something about the avalanche of ignored work still on my desk. A few days' interest on a few judgments would not break a multinational bank. But that wasn't the point: I was supposed to save my clients money. I was supposed to be a lawyer.

I knew what I'd encounter at work: the embarrassed silence of colleagues who'd seen me shrieking at yesterday's press conferences, live or on the eleven-o'clock news; the pill-shaking ire of Doron White; wary inquiries from conservative clients. And of course the usual: frantic phone calls from men with collateral at risk,

94 Lia Matera

threats parried in briefs and in hallways and in court-
rooms, sizzling frustration with stupid judges and incompetent word processors, legal arguments that
wouldn't hang together no matter how much money was
at stake.

I crossed the reception area of the office suite at ten
minutes to eight. I walked quickly. I wasn't handling
adversity well. I could handle my job.

As I entered the corridor, I spied the partners through
the open conference-room door. Six of them, in varying
states of anger or gloom, perusing copies of some doc-
ument. One of them caught sight of me and gestured to
Doron White. White rose and walked deliberately to
the door. He closed it in my face.

I sat in my office without doing much of anything.
After six years, they might have had the decency to
speak their minds rather than shut me out.

Eventually, I read through my telephone messages.
Most of them were from reporters. I put them in a tidy
pile. Maybe I'd call them later. Depending on what the
partners were plotting, I might not have anything to
lose.

The remaining messages were either business calls or
calls from friends of Crosetti.

Of the latter, there were three: one from Keith Asimov, one from Barbara Nottata, and one from Mark
Bresenzcy, which my secretary had subtitled "lawyer
from Clearinghouse."

Doron White opened my door and stepped in. He
looked around the room as if measuring it for new rugs.

He did not sit. He said, "I warned you yesterday that
I would convene a partners' meeting to discuss your use
of office facilities for an unauthorized press conference."

White dared hope Crosetti's death would be the end of our power struggle. He'd taken my press conference like a knife in the back.

"No authorization has ever been required for use of office space on a client-related matter." I wearily repeated yesterday's line of defense.

"Mr. Crosetti ceased to be a client when he, um, ceased to be. You can hardly claim to represent an interest that did not survive him."

White looked ashen and pinched, as drab as his mouse-gray suit. He pulled out the heart pills, looking, for once, as if he might really need them.

"I have been advised to take a brief vacation." His eyes glittered with anger or self-pity. "I came in today because I strongly believed the partners' meeting should not be delayed. Especially not"—he paused to hyperventilate—"after seeing your display on last night's news."

I felt myself flush. Easy to be snide about this prissy man, but he had a legitimate grievance. The disgrace was not mine alone; it reflected on the firm White had spent thirty years building. "I'm sorry, Doron. Dan Crosetti died right in front of me. He was a friend of mine—an innocent man. I was very upset."

It was the most personal remark I'd made to White in six years of sharing office space. He did not appear honored.

"We have prepared a letter of termination. It outlines for you the dates upon which you were put on notice of—and ignored!—the wishes of the partners of this firm. It explains fully and I think satisfactorily the reasons for your dismissal."

Dismissal. Oh God. "Effective when?"

"Effective immediately. We have prepared a termination package that includes six months' severance pay.''

Six months—far more than customary. The firm would lose over a thousand billable hours of my time— $185,000 in lost income. Plus the eighty-some thousand in severance pay.

I had no idea White wanted me out so badly. No idea he set my nuisance value so high.

I hit back: ''My clients don't care where I hold my press conferences, Doron. All they know is I win their motions. I could take half a dozen bank clients out of here with me, if I wanted to.''

Doron's lips pinched to the point of eclipse. His nostrils flared and his head shook, but he said nothing.

''Doron—'' A note of pleading. ''I was looking for a partnership—not a golden parachute.''

''Partnership?'' An explosion of incredulity. ''A partnership is a team. You're not a team player. You're a prima donna, and we've put up with—''

''Prima donna! You're the one who called me back from vacation to take the law-school-murders case, Doron—don't forget. If I've gotten a lot of attention, it's been incidental to my cases—part of doing my job. Nothing I planned.''

He squinted down at me. ''If you want to get ugly about this, Laura, fine. But after the irresponsible, possibly libelous things you said yesterday—in public!—I don't think anybody will blame us for removing your name from the letterhead.''

Probably not. ''I won't go gracefully, Doron.''

''So long as you go today.''

15

My secretary, Rose, came in crying. She'd been ordered not to put calls through to me. It took a little bracing rudeness to get her out of my office. She deserved better, and I knew it. She was worried about me and worried about her own job. Some people become generous and empathetic in adversity. I guess I don't.

I surveyed the stacks of files and transcripts and interrogatories and loan documents on my desk. It seemed unnatural not to work on them. I buzzed Rose. "I want a complete list of every case I've worked on over the last six years and an alphabetical index of the clients."

"Is it okay if they see me doing it?" Her voice was whispery over the speaker.

"Just do it. If anyone gives you any grief, send him in here." Terminated "effective immediately." I supposed I wasn't entitled to give her orders anymore.

Her voice hushed almost to inaudibility. "There are some people out in reception that I think came to see

you. Mr. White is talking to them. There's a lot of
noise. I think he's sending them away.''

Probably reporters. White was probably doing me a
favor. Nevertheless—

I walked past Rose's office to the reception desk. The
young butterfly of a receptionist was immobile with
shock, fluttering her eyelids and staring at the door.

There, apparently getting a polite version of the bum's
rush, were three of Crosetti's friends from the Clearinghouse.

Keith Asimov stood almost nose to nose with White,
his neck thrust forward like a lizard in a territorial dis-
pute. Two steps behind him were Barbara Nottata and
Mark Bresenzcy, looking equally determined, if less
belligerent.

Asimov was saying, ''My business with her is *my*
business! Where do you get off saying—''

''I am attempting to explain''—Doron White clutched
his pill bottle through the fabric of his suit pocket—
''that Ms. Di Palma is no longer associated with us.''

''Bullshit!'' Asimov raged. ''When I left a message
for her—''

''If you're here to see me''—I had to speak loudly to
be heard—''please come into my office.''

White wheeled around. He was red-faced, his eyes
were round. He glanced at me, then at the astonished
young receptionist. Public showdowns were not his
style. He withdrew to a marble sideboard, poking his
finger into a silver platter of foil-wrapped Godivas.

I gestured for the threesome to follow me. Damn Do-
ron! Turning away my clients and stopping my calls.
Did he really think he could keep me incommunicado?
Hustle me out the back door?

I led Danny's friends to my office and waved them

into the red leather chairs. I sat at my desk, pushing back papers that were no longer my concern.

I knew what these people wanted. They wanted the details of Dan Crosetti's death, an eyewitness account of the pathos and the gore; something to hold on to, something more real than a glib newspaper story.

It was the last thing in the world I wanted to talk about, but I guess they were entitled.

Barbara Nottata broke the silence. "We saw you on the news. We were glad you spoke up for Danny."

I blinked at her. With her polished nails and pressed corduroy jacket, she looked like she'd been out in the real world. Was she really pleased by my ineffective outburst?

She looked a little disconcerted; maybe I was broadcasting my hostility. "Anyway, we wanted to offer our services."

Inheriting Danny's gofers. I nearly laughed.

Mark Bresenzcy squared his narrow shoulders and added, "I'd be happy to do legal research for you. I took the bar exam in July again. A lot's still fresh in my mind. I don't know anything about the Freedom of Information Act, but I could find out if there's any way to get Dan's file from the FBI."

He'd taken the bar exam? Maybe he did have a skill to put at my disposal.

I reached for my yellow pad, and jotted down some statute numbers and case names. "Start here. I think only the subject of an investigation has the right to petition to look at his file. But see if the courts have said anything about a deceased's representative—lawyer or next-of-kin—having access."

I tore off the sheet and leaned across my desk to hand it to him. He rose from a leather chair and took the paper. Distracted, he backed into the hardwood chair, gasping as the zigzag arm goosed him.

"I had some clerks working on how to get information about Lefevre. That's probably pie in the sky now that we don't have an active criminal—" I faltered, shuffling files again.

Mark Bresenzcy sidled back to the leather chair. "If you tell me who to talk to, I'll find out where they left off."

"In our law library—ask for Sarah or Peter." The files in front of me were labeled *Investment Counseling Group v. Smoot and Does; Second Continental Bank v. Borstmann Properties; Hickman, Lyman, Peterson v. Bay Coast Factor.* Did I really want to woo these clients away from Doron White?

Barbara Nottata spoke, a little hesitantly. "Actually, I was thinking I might also be able to help. I was a nurse for quite a few years."

I looked up from the files to find her watching me carefully, head inclined. Did I look sick? "I'm not sure what . . . ?"

"If there's any question about the way Dan died? I could help you interpret the coroner's record."

"It'll be at least a week before the reports are filed. *If* they've finished the microscopy and toxicology work." And I wouldn't need any damn help interpreting the reports. I already knew what they'd say.

"But the autopsy? That's certainly been done."

"Yes. Look . . ." It would be nice to believe someone had walked in off the street and killed Dan Crosetti. It was more painful to consider his mounting torment and deprivation; to see Danny's suicide as the last domino in an eighteen-year chain. "He killed himself. There's really no doubt." Did I owe them the details?

Asimov seemed to think so. "How can you know that for sure? We saw him a couple of hours before!" With a shaking hand he swept a broad arc. "He was making plans. He was—"

"That's right," Barbara nodded. "Contingency plans."

The young lawyer pursed his lips in apparent disapproval.

"For going underground?" My pep talk obviously hadn't inspired optimism. All the more reason to believe Danny had killed himself.

Asimov slid forward on his chair. "Can we trust you? I mean, is this privileged, what we say to you?"

"No. You're not my clients."

More to the point, I didn't want the information. What good would it do, hearing about desperate alternatives Danny had rejected?

"Please don't tell me anything that implicates you or anyone else in any illegality. I'd be obligated to tell the police."

"They can't put Danny in jail now," Barbara said. "We can trust her."

Mark Bresenzcy shook his head. "There's no point in—"

"Yes, there is!" Barbara's voice carried conviction without rising in decibels. "We need to pool our information. Something might come out of it."

Asimov fixed me with a bright stare. "I don't want to mention any other names, but Danny was mapping things out. Getting ready to split. He and Barbara talked about it in detail"—he paused to allow her time to nod—"and I can guarantee when I talked to him he wasn't thinking about suicide."

"Ms. Di Palma?" Bresenzcy sounded almost deferential. "If you'd talked to him, you'd find the suicide scenario hard to believe, too."

"But I did talk to him. I talked to him through the bathroom door while he was dying." I pushed away from my desk. "What do you want from me? What kind of proof do you want?"

Barbara Nottata spoke calmly. "What did he say to you?"

"Jesus *Christ*!"

"If you don't tell us, we'll never know." Direct in its grief and frustration.

They were Danny's friends, closer to him than I'd ever been.

"When I went in there—" I felt my teeth grit; had to force myself to continue. "When Danny went under and I pulled his face out of the bath water, he said, 'Let go.' When he realized I'd called an ambulance he said, 'Oh, no.' He wanted to die; there's no doubt—"

Barbara Nottata interrupted. "I was an emergency-room nurse for two years. Blood loss can make people light-headed. What they say doesn't always relate to what's happening around them."

"I talked to him through the door for five or ten minutes. He was perfectly coherent. He didn't ask for help." How much did I owe these people, anyway? "Look, you don't want to hear it, but—"

"Dying people behave in bizarre ways!" She blushed, looking down at her folded hands. "We're not trying to deny your first-hand knowledge, it's just that it contradicts ours."

"Could we ask"—again Bresenzcy's tone was apologetic—"was *everything* in there consistent with suicide?"

"Yes! Believe me!" I looked at them one by one,

trying to will them to accept it. Barbara met my gaze with a slight shake of the head. Bresenzcy bit his lip and squinted. Asimov scowled in open disbelief.

"There was absolutely nothing inconsistent or wrong or off key?" Barbara leaned forward. "Nothing at all?"

Oh, God. What would they make of it? "One thing. His crutches and prosthesis. They weren't in the bathroom. And his wheelchair was in the hall."

For a moment they were as still as a mural; an improbable threesome in chairs that usually held bankers and lawyers.

"How did Danny get to the bathtub?" Barbara asked the question as if seriously expecting an answer.

The others waited, apparently also expecting an explanation. "I have no idea. I wouldn't bring it up if I did."

"Were his clothes in the bathroom?"

"No."

"So he went in nude?"

"Presumably."

"Were there slivers?" Spots of color appeared in her cheeks. "Have you talked to the medical examiner?"

Slivers. Crosetti's floorboards were exposed. If Danny dragged himself nude across the floor—

"You're a nurse? Here in town?"

"I *was* a nurse. In Iowa." She leaned closer. "Even if the coroner hasn't released the autopsy record, the medical examiner will talk to *you*—you were Danny's lawyer. He'll tell *you* if there were slivers." She was half a tone away from pleading.

"All right. Yes. I'll ask him." I already had an appointment with him. But slivers; I hadn't thought of that.

"Because if there weren't any slivers—" She gripped

the arms of the chair. "What you said yesterday at the DA's press conference? About how terrible it is that the Lefevre investigation is 'inactive'? Could you use this to make the police reopen the case? To create some doubt?"

I felt myself nod. Danny had killed himself; there was no question in my mind. But depending on what the medical examiner had to say, I might be able to raise a cloud of doubt. Until the police accounted for the crutches and proved Danny's suicide, they would have to keep the Lefevre investigation alive. No more of this "active-inactive" bullshit.

16

THE LAST THING I needed was a slow procession of associates through my office. I sat there all morning and most of the afternoon, answering glum questions, enduring nervous sympathy, and reassuring everyone that I expected no acts of protest on my behalf. (And a lot of good it would have done me if I had.) It was like being at my own wake.

I stifled the urge to flee for two reasons. The first was the client list Rose was typing for me. I had no idea what I would do with it, but I would make sure Doron White knew I had it.

The second was the medical examiner. I had a four-o'clock appointment with him, and I wanted to be in my office if he called before then. I wanted to be completely and unassailably official in my request for information. My alternative was to wait at least another week, until his reports were written and filed and available to the public.

By three-thirty, I had the case and client list in hand, and I'd given Rose an inventory of things in my office that belonged to me. If White, Sayres & Speck wanted me to parachute out, they could pack my damn bag for me. I tossed my Rolodex into my briefcase and said good-bye to what I'd thought would be a lifelong niche.

I waved to Rose as I walked by her office. I hurried through the reception room before she could jump up and water me with tears, before she could bring out a coterie of word processors or raise the alarm among the associates; before my leave-taking turned into another chorus of testimonials and vague lunch dates.

Or maybe I just like to think it would have.

In any case, it seemed appropriate that I was going to the morgue.

17

THE CORONER'S OFFICE was the usual down-at-the-heels, yellow-gray government office. Two deputy coroners sat at desks behind a long counter, looking grumpily official in matching blue slacks, white shirts, and blue ties. The back of the long room was lined with filing cabinets and shelves of coroner's records, bound by year of death. One of the two men was on the phone, snapping, "Go ahead—call my supervisor!"

His co-worker watched him, ignoring me.

The deputy slammed down the receiver, grumbling, "He's dead! What am I supposed to do—deliver him in a pizza carton?"

The co-worker twitched back a smile, finally stepping up to the counter. "What can I do for you?"

"I have an appointment with Dr. Stiglitz."

He craned his neck as if scanning the veldt. Fifteen feet away, in a glass-walled enclosure, a tall man with horn rims and a striped yellow shirt rose from his chair. The deputy beckoned to him.

A moment later, Dr. Stiglitz opened a door and welcomed me to the world behind the counter. Except for areas marked "Absolutely No Public Admittance" and a faint smell of phenol, it might have been any government office.

The doctor led me past cabinets stacked with files and memos, and into his cubicle. His desk was littered with photographs of wounds.

"Have a seat, Miss Di Palma." His belt buckle said *Spokane Expo '74* and a half-dozen pens filled his shirt pocket.

I knew Dr. Stiglitz slightly from my last criminal case. He was a nerdily cordial man, willing to explain every nick and bruise in loving detail. He smiled at me shyly, running a hand over cowlicks in his graying hair.

I sat in an armless vinyl chair. "I understand you've already autopsied Dan Crosetti."

Stiglitz nodded. "We're not quite done with the laboratory and toxicology work. But basically—" He shrugged, seating himself behind the littered desk. "The cause of death was exsanguination. He sliced his wrists." Stiglitz pantomimed transverse slits with his own wrist and finger. "Three times each side. Progressively deeper."

I glanced away, at a photo taped to the wall. Realizing it was a hugely swollen bite mark, I looked back at Stiglitz's face. "I'm wondering if you found any slivers in his body."

"Well, we were more or less expecting to." He raised his brows. "Or at least some detritus from the floorboards, but um—" He shrugged. "Dirt embedded in the epidermis could have soaked out into the bathwater.''

"But the floor's so rough—wouldn't he have gotten *some* slivers? In addition to dirt?"

"I'd say probability was on that side. But it's possible to suppose not, or to suppose the embedded material soaked out.''

"If it soaked out, wouldn't there have been residue in the bathtub?''

"Possibly. Or in the drain and the trap.''

"Did you find anything like that?''

"Nothing to speak of. But quite a volume of water went down the drain. It might have washed down.''

"When I pulled the plug''—God, I hated to think about it—"I was holding his head. As soon as the water was low enough, I put him down and went to call the ambulance. Wouldn't—'' Stiglitz looked interested; how could he stand a job composed of grizzly descriptions and grizzlier sights? "Wouldn't things get trapped in his hair?''

Stiglitz looked as pleased as a professor regarding a bright student. "We did comb out his hair and beard, looking for detritus.''

"Did you find anything?''

He frowned. "Well, yes and no. Not to the extent we'd have expected. Some grit that may have been on the floor because it was on Crosetti, rather than the other way around. But you know, what goes down a drain depends on where it's floating when the plug's pulled.''

"But you've clearly given it serious thought. It obviously concerned you.'' And I could use that concern to my advantage.

"Oh yes. We vacuumed and took several scrapings

of the bathroom floor before we allowed anyone to walk on it.''

In San Francisco, the coroner's office has exclusive control over the scene of a death. Even cops need permission to go in.

"Where did you find the crutches?''

"In Mr. Crosetti's bedroom.''

"Were they fingerprinted?''

A lopsided smile. "Oh, yes. And I've seen the report. All the prints are Mr. Crosetti's.''

"All of them?''

He nodded.

"But I saw someone handling those crutches the day before he died.''

"Interesting.'' He jotted down the information.

"Where were Crosetti's prints?''

"On the cross braces. Where you put your hands.''

"But not on the other parts? He had to handle the other parts to pick up the crutches.''

"Well, I think the assumption is that rubbing the crutches between the upper arm and chest—as you would, in general use—obliterated other prints.''

"But how did Crosetti put the crutches aside to get into his wheelchair? He has to have taken them by the—''

"He might have let them drop. We found them on the floor.''

Still, no fingerprints at all—it was another piece of information to throw into the confusion I planned to brew.

"Have you unsealed Crosetti's apartment?'' The "seal" consisted of a printed sign nailed to the door. But it had the force of law behind it; it was a misdemeanor to open a "sealed" door, a felony to touch anything inside.

"Technically, no. But we're through in there. As far as we're concerned, it can come down. I'll send someone out there later."

I considered this helpful, awkwardly brilliant man. As long as the coroner's seal was on that door, William Stiglitz had complete control of the scene. If he said I could go in, it didn't make a bit of difference whether the cops agreed or the landlord approved. Stiglitz could cut a lot of red tape for me.

"May I go in and look around?"

"Well." Stiglitz tilted his head and twitched his nose. "I don't see why not."

"Can I go through Crosetti's belongings?" The coroner's deputies had certainly looked for and failed to find a suicide note. They'd found and photographed the crutches. They'd done what they needed to do to the bath. What was left to disturb?

The medical examiner frowned. "You'd tell us anything you thought might have some bearing?"

"Of course."

"I'll find you a key." He shrugged. "Be sure to sign in and out."

18

IT WAS A cold, windy evening, the kind that reminds you Indian summer is over. Up the block, someone was cooking with hot spices. The smell of chili blended with the curb smell of wine and urine, the fishy, rusty smell of old shipyards. Somewhere in the neighborhood, a Baptist church had finished its evening service. Black women in 1950s coats and pillbox hats walked together, discussing a better world than the one that had ruined their children.

I pulled a pen out of my handbag and scribbled my name and the time on the last empty line of the coroner's seal. There were several entries above mine: coroner's deputies, cops, the deputy DA, an FBI agent, more coroner's deputies, more cops, another FBI agent. A sign-up sheet for vultures. I'd have to ask Stiglitz if the Feds had removed anything.

I fit the key Stiglitz had given me into Crosetti's door. It took an effort of will to turn it. What the hell was I doing here, anyway? Hadn't today been traumatic enough?

I finally stepped inside for the same reason I'd stepped in yesterday: a crowd of young black men walking briskly toward me.

Danny's apartment was dark, with bedsheet curtains nailed over the windows. In the waning light, the bars could be seen in depressing silhouette.

I clicked on a lamp, watching heat from the bulb raise a fine fur of cobwebs on the shade. The braided rug had been rolled up, and papers of various kinds, sizes, and colors had been stacked on the floor. Other than that, the living room looked almost undisturbed.

I tried not to think about the bathroom.

I sat on the floor beside the stacks of paper and began looking through them. Though previous visitors had obviously tried to organize them, they were too varied and eclectic for easy categorization. There was literature from two dozen alliances, political parties, and nonprofit organizations. There were newspaper and magazine clippings on many subjects: labor and immigration issues, environmental issues, gay and health-care issues, militarism at home and in Central America, social services and budget cutbacks. There were science and technical-journal articles about brown lung, acid rain, pesticide residues, food irradiation, the greenhouse effect, biological and chemical warfare.

I looked at my newsprint-blackened fingertips. No wonder Danny had been depressed.

I stood up, glancing around the room. It was a landlord's nightmare, a thousand thumbtack holes in walls that had probably sported a changing cycle of posters and agendas.

I stepped into the hallway, relieved to find the bathroom door closed. Whatever information I could gain from going in there I would do without.

I took a fast look around the kitchen. Dan Crosetti had lived on beans and rice, government-surplus cheese and powdered milk. Most of the food was in glass jars, safe from mice, roaches, and rats.

It reminded me of the way Hal had lived three years ago, in a condemned house with no electricity or water, his food similarly protected from pests.

With both men, it had been a matter of philosophy as well as necessity. I closed the cupboards, fighting revulsion. I didn't think I could do it, didn't think I could sacrifice convenience to conscience.

I spent about an hour in Danny's bedroom, standing at his desk (the only chair in the room was his wheelchair), looking through papers far more personal than anything in the living room. Everything was neatly filed. There was a file for each of Danny's arrests—indictments, court transcripts, appeals, newspaper articles. Ten of them in all. Four years and three months in prison for everything from counseling draft resistance to unlawful assembly. The arrests ranged in locale from Mississippi to Washington, D.C., to San Francisco. Locally, Danny had been represented by the legendary leftist Julian Warneke.

There were also thick files of correspondence that made me mourn Danny's passion and sensitivity, letters that crackled with intelligence and anger. Why hadn't I made a point of knowing Dan Crosetti better while he was alive?

But something was conspicuously missing, despite frequent mention of it in the letters: Crosetti's FBI records, obtained for him by Julian Warneke in 1983 and 1987 under the Freedom of Information Act.

Either Danny kept the records elsewhere—the Clearinghouse, perhaps?—or the FBI had removed them from the apartment.

19

I CLOSED MY eyes and my bedroom seemed to swirl as if I were being flushed down a drain.

I rewound my message casette, fast-forwarding over reporters' requests for statements and information (including why White, Sayres & Speck claimed I was no longer with the firm). I finally reached the right spot on the tape. And there was Hal's voice:

"Laura?" Background noise: voices, music—probably a bar. Someone asking, *Got it?* "You're probably taking a lot of shit about what you"—a garbled word or two, drowned out by a hoot of background laughter—"Crosetti. I saw it on TV. I don't say this very often; not as often as"—more inaudible words—"thought you did fine. Crosetti deserved a departure from the usual horseshit." A long pause. Even the background noise grew quieter. "Oh, God."

That was all. A few words of unexpected approval. And a despairing, "Oh, God."

My machine continued spewing out messages. A woman saying, "Susan Yen, Channel 33. I was at the press conference. Do you remember me from an interview after the verdict in—" I clicked it off, seeing, in a blink of the mind's eye, an Asian woman in a red suit.

Hal might be coherent again (thank God), but he wasn't all right. His voice was labored, weary, tentative. I remembered his unsteady progress across the rehabilitation-room floor, the confusion in his eyes—Jesus, only five days ago. Where was he sleeping now? How was he finding food?

I pulled the tape out of the machine, dropping it twice before I got my trembling under control. Couldn't Hal understand? I'd thought he needed care; I wasn't trying to force it on him. Bad enough to pay for your mistakes without having to pay for your good intentions, too.

I looked around the bedroom, loathing every hand-stitched eyelet in the comforter, every shimmer in the oiled wainscot. My modest opulence offended Hal. To Danny, it must have seemed obscene.

God, I hoped there was more to me than the sum of my possessions.

I slipped the casette tape into my suit pocket and replaced it with a blank. Almost immediately the phone rang, and my message began to play.

As soon as I heard a stranger's voice respond to the beep, I left the bedroom. I went out looking for Hal.

20

I STOOD UNDER a street lamp on the loop that wound past the sphinxes of the de Young Museum, the pruned grove of the Music Concourse, the scrubbed columns of the Academy of Sciences. Fog tumbled past streetlamps, museum flags snapped. I shivered in my linen suit, listening to hedges stir and twigs crack.

I knew there were hundreds of homeless people camped in Golden Gate Park, hiding in shrubs, huddling in tunnels, moving from one spot to another as telltale bits of litter betrayed their homes to gardeners. In the morning, there were rows of them lying under cold sprinklers to get clean. In the afternoon, they could be seen pilfering chili dogs from dumpsters.

Hal might be one of them.

I'd encountered him here in 1981; encountered him on the spot where I now stood.

I'd been on my way to the de Young when I recognized Hal's voice in the snide greeting, "Little Laura."

118

Hal's voice coming from a much older man in worn jeans and a stretched-out sweater. A man climbing out of a rusty and decrepit van.

I'd taken a step toward him. A long look before I could make myself believe it. I remember saying, "Where the hell have you been?"

It had been a regular lament of my papa's that his second cousin's son should stay gone for years without so much as a postcard. "What did Henry do to his son to deserve such a slap in the face?" Pointing to my "Uncle" Henry's myriad civic projects and my "Aunt" Diana's unceasing luncheons and fêtes, I'd always replied, "They don't give a damn."

"Where have I been?" Hal's response had been dryly delivered. "I've been enjoying a hero's welcome. And yourself?"

Looking up at Hal, at his bristling haircut and tired face, I'd known I wouldn't mention the encounter to my papa. What could I say? That what had begun with Hal's refusal to drive the sports car unveiled before photographers on his sixteenth birthday had ended with him in an ancient van in Golden Gate Park?

Now, I felt icy tears on my cheeks. Tears again, damn it.

"I didn't want to put you in that place, Hal. The doctor said the first two weeks were critical. That if I didn't— that if you didn't recover within—"

A car turned off Kennedy Drive, catching me in its headlights. I blinked and stepped back, preparing to dash to my Mercedes.

"You're crazy as a coot, you know that?" the driver called out.

"Sandy."

"What the hell are you doing out here?" He slid

from behind the driver's seat, slamming the door of a three-year-old Buick chosen because it was inconspicuous.

"How did you know where—?"

He strode quickly toward me, silhouetted by his headlights. "You've been cruising the park every night since Hal— Jesus God, Laura! The park's fifty blocks long and eight blocks deep. What are the odds?"

He gripped my shoulders. For a second I thought he was going to shake me.

I could see the outline of his lean body, slouched so he could peer at my face. I closed my eyes, as if that would make the tears invisible.

"Hell, Laura." His tone was gentler than his words. "If Hal wanted you to find him, he'd go to your apartment—he wouldn't go someplace you happened to run into him years ago."

"Did you get my message? Did you play the tape?"

"Yes. And I'll tell you something, there's a lot of bars in town, but you'd be smarter going to every fucking one of them than standing out here in the—" The last vestige of exasperation left his voice. "Come on, sweetheart. Let's go someplace warm and talk. Have you eaten anything today?"

"No." I looked at him. Hated the pity I saw on his face, and looked away, at unearthly sphinxes glowering in the lamplight.

Sandy cupped my chin in his hand, turning my face up to his. In the misty light, he looked like an old movie. Gary Cooper as Mr. Deeds. He folded me into his arms.

We stood like that awhile, then I let him walk me to the Buick.

21

IT WAS ALMOST midnight when I got home. Pushing around a few forkfuls of pasta hadn't improved my mood.

The first thing I did was check my telephone messages.

There were only a few of them: reporters were diurnal. No message from Hal.

I dialed SFPD's Homicide Detail and asked to speak to Inspector Krisbaum. "He left a message for me to return his call as soon as possible."

A harried voice replied, "One moment," and clicked me into soundless hold.

What the hell did Homicide want with me? Peeved that I'd poked around Crosetti's apartment? That I hadn't asked their permission? Well, tough.

Krisbaum came on the line. "Miss Di Palma? Inspector Daniel Krisbaum here. Thank you for returning my call."

"My pleasure." Jesus.

"I'd like to speak with you this evening."

"This evening?" What side of midnight were we on? "As in several hours from now?"

"No, actually I meant right now. I realize it's late. If you prefer not to drive, I'd be glad to come and get you." His voice seemed to brook no third alternative.

"What's this about?"

"If we could discuss it in person—"

"No."

A weary sigh. "I'd rather call it a night, too, Miss Di Palma. But I'm afraid this won't keep."

"Look, I had the coroner's permission to go to Dan Crosetti's apartment—you can check with Dr. Stiglitz. And I was told the seal was coming off—that's why I didn't return the key."

"This isn't about Dan Crosetti."

"Then—"

"All right. I don't blame you—it is late. Here's my problem. Last two hours, we've been in your office—"

"My *office*? Why?"

"Doron White. I gather he was the senior partner—"

"Of my law firm. What about him?"

"Well. He's dead."

I sank onto my bed, closing my eyes. I could see Doron sitting on the Art Deco chair gripping his bottle of medication, all but accusing me of triggering his heart attack. I heard myself whisper, "Shit."

"It looks like a heart attack—we found nitroglycerin pills in his pocket. But he was in your office, and uh . . . We thought we'd like to talk to you." His tone was almost coaxing.

"Why?" I felt a flame of guilt—I'd always ignored White's security-blanket grip on those pills; never allowed his heart condition to influence what I did or said to him. "I didn't trigger the heart attack."

"The thing is, he was in your office, and—"

"Doing what?"

"That's why I thought we should talk, Miss Di Palma. We think a heart attack carried him away, but he had some help getting there."

I leaped to my feet. Since when did Homicide harass people for contributing to the stress of heart-attack victims?

"Listen." Krisbaum sounded miffed. "I might as well quit beating around the bush. White was roughed up."

"Roughed . . . ?" It seemed an impossible violation of Doron's dignity. Impossible to imagine and impossible to believe.

"Your car or mine, Miss Di Palma?"

22

I T WAS TWO-THIRTY in the morning. In the middle of my office, a man unplugged a hand-held lamp. Without its purplish light, a roomful of glowing fingerprints faded from view. At my desk, another man labeled tape-lifted prints and noted their location on a schematic sketch of the office. I looked down at my own fingers, still slick from the towelette I'd used to wipe off fingerprint ink. The chair on which I sat showed traces of graphite powder on its leather arm.

I added a few names to the yellow legal pad on my knee, glancing up at the Homicide inspector. "These are the staff people that came in today." I'd already listed the attorneys and the few clients I'd seen that week. "The only other people I remember coming in here were friends of Dan Crosetti's." I added Keith Asimov, Mark Bresenzcy, and Barbara Nottata to the list. "Friends from the Clearinghouse for Peace."

Krisbaum knelt beside me, squinting at my ignore-the-lines scrawl. "Okay. We'll get prints from these people and start our process of elimination."

Process of elimination—who did he think he was kidding? He wasn't expecting to find any other prints. Why would a stranger sneak into my office and rough up Doron White?

No, Krisbaum thought I'd done it. He'd thought so the minute he spotted my duplicate list of personal possessions on the blotter. The minute he learned White had fired me without notice. That's why I was sitting here in the middle of the night, enduring his Columbo routine.

And, I had to admit, from Krisbaum's point of view it made sense. Who was more likely to come to the office after most people had gone home? More likely to draw White into the room, spark an argument and lose control? Who was more likely to lash out than a woman summarily dismissed half a year away from partnership?

"I can't tell you anything more, Inspector. I left the office at three-thirty. You know where I went after that."

Krisbaum tore the list off the legal pad. "Yes, all right. Thanks—you've been very cooperative."

"You sound surprised."

"Well, your reputation—"

"I'm not acting on a client's behalf."

A reluctant grin. "I see."

I rose, smoothing my shirt into my waistband. Jesus, my stomach hurt.

"We'll probably need something more formal in the way of a statement tomorrow—or rather, later today." He gestured to a uniformed cop. "Drive Miss Di Palma home."

I stopped at the door and took a last look around my

office. Art Deco desk, abstract chair, giant collages, yards of red leather. I hoped I'd remember it without the blacklight fingerprints and the chalk marks where White had fallen. I hoped I'd remember it without the fingerprint tape and the coroner's deputy wiping surfaces for bits of hair and scalp.

Sure.

23

I LOOKED AT my wall clock, a slab of black glass confettied with turquoise and fuchsia squares. The hands were wavy yellow lines, hard to see from the couch. Very hard to see—at what, seven-thirty?—after a night of pacing and crying. But I must have gotten some sleep—the doorbell woke me.

Who the hell would come over this early? Police? Sandy? Someone from the office?

I slid my stockinged legs off the couch and pulled down my skirt. One thing about sleeping in your clothes, you don't have to rush to get dressed. I ran my fingers through my hair and padded to the front door. I looked through the peephole: not many people I'd admit at this hour and in this condition.

It was Barbara Nottata. She was apparently conscious of being watched through the fisheye. She mouthed the word "Please," and held up two thick files.

My eyes burned, my sinuses stung, my head ached. I undoubtedly looked like hell.

But I opened the door to Dan Crosetti's friend.

Barbara wore pressed jeans, shined penny loafers, and a Fair Isles sweater, unstretched and without pills. Her hair was smoothly high on top, clipped into feminine sideburns. No makeup, but shaped brows and creamed skin. A careful compromise between vanity and comfort.

"I'm sorry. I know it's early." She seemed startled by my dishabille; kept her eyes politely on my face. "I thought you'd be leaving for work soon."

"Not today."

"And I was excited about this." She held up two files, each containing an inch of documents. "It took me most of yesterday to find them, and I knew you'd want to see them."

The last was almost a question.

"Come in."

She stepped in hesitantly. "They're Danny's FBI files. Two sets—one that goes up to nineteen-eighty-three and one from eighty-three to eighty-seven." She handed them to me.

"Where did you get them?"

"The Clearinghouse. I went through about forty boxes yesterday."

If I'd been operating on a level approaching rationality, I'd have had Sandy do that the night Danny died.

I waved her into a chair, the deep-cushioned one Danny'd had to struggle out of. "Give me a few minutes to wash up."

I carried the file folders back to the bedroom with me, flipping quickly through the topmost. It was full of murkily Xeroxed FBI memoranda, each with dozens of lines blacked out. The FBI is not obligated to reveal its sources, or—a major loophole—any information from which a source's identity might be inferred.

I set the folders down beside the answering machine and played back my messages. Three from early-bird reporters, and two from associates at White, Sayres & Speck. Had they heard about Doron so soon?

I erased the messages. Let them talk to each other.

I shucked my suit and took a quick hot shower. Put on corduroy pants and an angora sweater, suede flats. Soft clothes, for psychic comfort.

When I went back out to the living room, Barbara Nottata was no longer in the down chair. I could smell coffee.

I found her in my closet of a kitchen, pressing grounds to the bottom of a French press.

She looked a little sheepish. "Do you mind? Everything was pretty much out on the counter"—beans in the freezer, grinder in the cupboard, pot in the sink— "so I knew you must drink the stuff too."

I shrugged, reaching into a cupboard for the handmade mugs I'd been ashamed to display for Dan Crosetti.

"Milligans," Barbara murmured, filling them. "I have a Milligan teapot. One of his early ones, with the animals."

"I've probably got some food around here, if you're hungry."

"No. Thanks. I just need some coffee."

We carried the mugs out to the bay windows overlooking the Presidio. The table was a small circle of black marble, barely large enough to spread out the papers.

"Where did you find the files?" The coffee was joltingly strong. Suited to the task at hand.

Barbara sat forward, elbows on the marble. "The FBI came to the Clearinghouse—did anyone tell you? While we were at your office yesterday morning. They asked Tree where Danny kept his papers, and if they could take a look at them. Apparently they were very pleasant but very persistent. Tree's a mess today." She shook her head. "We all like to think we'd withstand torture before we offered information. But it's hard to withstand politeness."

"I take it Tree"—what a name—"showed them Danny's papers?"

Barbara frowned. "The FBI's been in before—they were there when the police searched for the rifle, right after Danny was arrested. And they've been back since, without any kind of warrant. But we always turned them away, me or Keith or Mark. So it's easy for Keith and the others to blame Tree, but . . ."

She shrugged. "Tree didn't expect the agents to be so nice, you know? She's young, very sweet—does the PeaceEd Resources coordinating. She said they didn't act like she had any choice, like it was a foregone conclusion they'd see the papers. And they kept reassuring her it was morally okay to show them. That they just wanted to see justice done—wouldn't be interested in Danny's papers if they thought he'd killed John Lefevre."

I felt my hands strangle the mug. They were so fucking smooth. "The FBI always knows the right buttons to punch. When I represented Wallace Bean, they went to his family members and said—" I forced myself to stop. If I started thinking about Bean—where my "success" on that case had led him (and me), I'd go crazy.

Barbara waited a few seconds, making sure I'd abandoned the subject. "Anyway, Tree showed them where Danny stored his papers. They took away six file boxes full."

"Shit!" Even posthumously, I'd let Danny down. "I should have moved them to my place day before yesterday."

She looked at me, face troubled, beginning to shake her head. Telling me the comrades wouldn't have allowed it?

"Well," she glanced away, "I doubt if there was anything very private in there. Not in boxes with Danny's name written on them. Not with all the traffic we get at the Clearinghouse."

"How long have you worked there?"

"Only four weeks—no, five."

"Long enough to know what kind of stuff Danny accumulated?"

"Well, Keith could tell you better than I can. But from what I saw going into his mailbox, it was mostly literature and memos."

"What kind of memos?"

"Steering committees. Danny was on a dozen steering committees, everything from United Campuses to Ploughshares."

"So the FBI got some memos. Strategy, game plans, that kind of thing?"

"Mostly rhetoric and self-criticism." She smiled wryly.

I sipped my coffee and watched her.

She continued more heatedly. "I don't see why the FBI needs Danny's papers when presumably John Lefevre told them everything Danny was doing!"

"Maybe Lefevre *didn't* tell them."

She blinked with surprise. "I, um, wondered—and the reason I looked through the boxes—I thought they must be looking for something in particular, something Lefevre hadn't found. And I couldn't believe"—she fingered the buttons on her Fair Isles yoke—"couldn't *believe* Danny would keep something private or sensitive—something he didn't even show John—in there with his other stuff."

"Danny had some expectation of privacy, didn't he? You don't let people go through each other's papers?"

"No." She flashed me a mischievous grin. "But I snooped yesterday—because nobody was around to stop me." Looking more serious: "Besides, Danny came to the Clearinghouse several times after John was killed. If he had any expectation of privacy before, it would have been gone by then. He'd have moved anything important—don't you think?"

"So you decided to look in other people's file boxes."

"Yes. It seemed more logical that he'd take stuff home, but . . ." She shrugged. "I thought I should give it a shot."

I tapped the emptied file folders. "And you found these."

She nodded. "With the Interfaith Counsel for Peace stuff. They're up in Oregon—they don't get down to San Francisco very often. They've got a couple of things in a dusty box labeled 'Out of State.' The files were in there."

"You didn't find anything else of Danny's?"

"No. I don't know—it all looks alike after a while. But this has Danny's name on it. I couldn't miss it. Maybe if Keith went through everything—"

"I'll send a detective over to help him."

"If Danny was planning"—she bit her lip—"to kill himself—"

"Why did he hide his files?"

We looked at one another across the paper-strewn marble.

"Let's hope they tell us something." I picked up the folder labeled "1965–83" and handed Barbara the one labeled "1983–87."

For the next half hour, we didn't speak. Barbara got up twice to refill our coffee cups. We traded files and continued reading. Twenty-two years of FBI reports headed, "Title: DANIEL MORELLI CROSETTI, Character: SECURITY MATTER—[here, any of a number of political organizations]—KEY ACTIVIST"; or "ACTING ASSISTANT ATTORNEY GENERAL, CRIMINAL DIVISION, [the date]— Re WIRETAPS"; or "CIA MEMORANDUM, To: DIRECTOR, FEDERAL BUREAU OF INVESTIGATION, From: DEPUTY DIRECTOR (PLANS)."

The early reports began with Danny's background— information pillaged from birth certificates, school transcripts, college financial-aid applications, health department records; and gossip from sources whose names and locations had been blacked out.

Later reports focused on Danny's organizing activities. FBI "Special Agents" (their names blacked out) related in stilted jargon what had transpired in hundreds of meetings and dozens of marches and even in the backs of a few paddy wagons. Seven cities and two decades' worth of "Source [name blacked out] further advised that Crosetti stated . . ." or "Subject spoke before audience of approximately . . ."

My respect for Dan Crosetti grew as I read this testimonial to his commitment—commitment to desegregating Mississippi's lunch counters, to ending the devastation of Vietnamese flesh and foliage, to easing the burdens of the homeless and the disabled.

At predictably regular intervals, CIA memoranda noted that organizations to which Danny had belonged—beginning with the NAACP and ending with Nuclear Watch—"are under investigation to discover clear linkage with the Communist Party of the United States and/or control by the international Communist movement."

I read through everything twice. It was a fascinating essay on the changing definition of "subversion," but it contained nothing unexpected, nothing to explain why Danny had secreted the files.

"Something's missing." I was surprised by how positive I sounded.

Barbara looked up from a file. "What?"

I stood, crossing to the window. I hammered it open with my fist, letting in a blast of eucalyptus-scented wind. "I don't know. I feel like my head's stuffed with cobwebs."

"Well"—she pushed the file away—"if it makes you feel any better, I can't figure out what it is, either."

"But you have the same feeling?"

She nodded.

"I looked through the papers he kept at home."

"Anything?" She shivered in her Irish wool.

"No. But the FBI got there before me." So did the cops, the coroner's deputies, and the deputy DA.

I leaned out the window, looking past the stone wall separating the narrow street from the Presidio's trees and lawns. In the distance a golf cart skirted a rise, flag flapping. A squirrel darted across the green.

Barbara Nottata observed, "You have a beautiful apartment. Beautiful view. A nice feeling to it."

I closed my eyes, inhaling mentholated wind. A nice feeling to it—I used to think so, too. High ceiling, white walls, interesting art, comfortable furniture. A place where you could see trees and smell grass. How guilty should I feel about it?

I turned back to her. "You devote a lot of time to the Clearinghouse, don't you?"

She rubbed her arms. "Relatively. Not like Keith."

"Did you always do that kind of thing?"

"No. It's hard when you're working full time."

"You're not working now?"

"No. I had kind of a—" She looked beyond me, at the fluttering gum trees. "Well, not to put too fine a point on it, I had a breakdown. Back in Iowa. I was working with AIDS patients, and that was pretty devastating. Then my husband"—her throat rippled as she swallowed quickly, several times—"left me."

"So you came out here?"

She nodded. "My sister needed a roommate. I had some money saved."

"Why the Clearinghouse?"

She looked into her coffee cup. "I'm told it's a fairly common reaction. If you're hurting, you have more empathy. It seems more important to help people."

"Christianity would have died without Nero?"

She smiled, getting a little pink of cheek. "Basically."

"You do some kind of counseling, don't you?"

"Sexual-assault victims, mostly." She frowned. "The nursing experience helps a lot with that. And, well . . . I'm still not ready to go back to working with AIDS patients. The assault victims, at least they're going to live through it." Tears sparkled in her eyes. "It helps me, too. It's like a context for my life. A way to do something—be worth something.''

I watched her blink back the tears. Flash an embarrassed smile. ''I like to think I'm not such a crybaby anymore. But sometimes . . .''

I turned away. Leaned my forehead on the window sash.

She murmured, ''Anyway, it's low-impact stuff compared to what you've been doing.''

I spoke to the street below. ''You think I've made an impact? I evolve a new defense in the Bean case, and the legislature's so outraged they outlaw it. I break ground on jury instructions in the law-school case, and I get sacks of hate mail for getting a murderer off with—'' I turned back to her. ''The only people I've helped are killers and bankers.'' I gestured toward our mugs. ''And a few potters and collage makers.''

''But you used to work at the Clearinghouse. Danny was telling us—''

''I was a kid then—nineteen. I'd just run away from my hometown. My husband—ex-husband now—had screwed me over.''

Her smile surprised me. ''Like me,'' she said. ''That's where I am right now.''

I sat back down. ''Look, tell me—what do you really know about John Lefevre? Not necessarily what he told you, but what you could see of his real personality. Did he fit into what we're talking about now? Did he strike you as a—'' I groped for the right word.

''Walking wounded?'' Her tone was ironic. Then she nodded thoughtfully. ''Yes, in a way, he did.''

''In what way?''

''I'm not sure I can put my finger on it. Things upset him—even though he didn't say anything, his complexion would change. He seemed a little . . . tender. Like he was bleeding around the edges." She blushed again. "Like me, I guess. Like you."

I ignored the last remark. "Before Lefevre was assigned to Crosetti, he took a six-month leave of absence. He lived on Clayton Street, off Haight. He did a lot of drugs."

"Drugs?" She shook her head. "I don't believe it. Not John Lefevre."

"That's what my detective tells me."

"Maybe John was just pretending, as part of his cover. Maybe he was on assignment."

"According to my detective, he was on leave of absence."

Barbara Nottata looked unconvinced. "It's hard to imagine the FBI letting an agent do that—take a leave of absence and get involved with drugs. And if John did do that, wouldn't the bureau find out? I don't know that much about the FBI, but . . . is your detective reliable?"

My detective—formerly my boyfriend—had run an elaborate game during a case we'd worked on together three years ago. I'd thought I was calling the shots, but it turned out Sander Arkelett had manipulated me every step of the way.

I'd let him get away with a felony. And he'd taken two bullets in the chest for me.

"I trust Sandy," I told her. "Completely."

24

I SPENT HALF an hour up in Homicide, supplying the "more formal" statement Krisbaum had requested. The interrogation rooms were in use, so I sat in the middle of the crowded, bustling main room, at one of many paired desks. The desk was coffee-ringed and cluttered and strewn with crumbs. It belonged to Inspector James Kelly, a beefy young man in a Missoni vest.

Kelly took patient notes as I repeated for him what I'd told Krisbaum hours before. Distractedly, I watched men in tacky suits rummage through files and make phone calls and joke with reporters and eat sandwiches at their desks. To my left, windows framed a tiered freeway roaring with morning traffic. In a glass-walled corner, San Francisco's beleaguered Homicide lieutenant sat with his head bowed, apparently enduring the aspersions of a petition-waving old man.

Doron White had been "roughed up." No doubt about it, Inspector Kelly informed me.

Roughed up. If the beating caused the heart attack, it was involuntary manslaughter. If Doron was manhandled by someone aware of his condition, it was more than that. It was murder.

Kelly laboriously transcribed the last of my answers, that I had noticed nothing unusual or out of place in my office last night. Then he sat back and grinned at me.

Krisbaum wouldn't have requested a formal statement unless he envisioned using it later to catch me in a lie. His partner knew the plan.

"Do me a favor, Mr. Kelly?" I'd done him one by coming here, hadn't I?

He waved expansively. Then, more sensibly, "If I can."

"Let me talk to the medical examiner who autopsied Doron White."

The grin vanished. His broad forehead puckered.

"Look, Inspector, there's nothing improper I can do with the information. You've got my statement literally in hand—you know I didn't go near Doron White last night. You know I'm not going to use the medical information as the basis of an accident or self-defense claim. And the autopsy report will be public information soon." In California, thirty dollars and a phone call will get you a complete coroner's report—anybody's—as soon as the investigation is closed. But I wanted the information today. Now. *Quid pro quo.*

Krisbaum would cease being surprised by my cooperativeness, but I could live with that.

Kelly gnawed his thumb indecisively. Finally he said, "How about you clear it with the lieutenant?"

I was afraid he might suggest that. Thank goodness I'd foreseen it. "I'll do that while you're typing the statement."

I threaded my way through knots of conferring males,

some in suits, some in uniforms, some (to my surprise) in baseball jerseys.

When I tapped the glass door labeled LIEUTENANT OF POLICE, HOMICIDE DETAIL, Lieutenant Don Surgelato looked up with obvious relief. Through the glass I could hear his visitor snap, "—little better than a boondoggle."

The lieutenant rose and gestured for me to enter.

As I opened the door, he said, "My next appointment is here. So if you'll just leave that on my desk, I'll get back to you."

The old man fixed me with a poisonous glare. He slapped the petition down, replying, "*If* you're still in this office."

Surgelato's olive skin grew darker. He was the subject of a well-financed, if not well-organized, attempt to get him fired. Several months earlier, he'd shot and killed the colorful—and inexplicably popular—murderer of Julian Warneke. Warneke, probably the nation's most famous left-wing lawyer, had represented Dan Crosetti many times. Danny would have chosen Warneke instead of me, if he'd had a choice. Small world.

Surgelato waited for the other man to leave. Then he turned his attention to me. He looked as Italian as his last name implied—compactly heavy, low hairline, dark eyes under thick brows, nose that was either broken or Calabrese. A type represented in my own family album.

I extended my hand. "Laura Di Palma. You may remember me from—"

"Never fear"—a sour smile—"I remember you very well, Ms. Di Palma." He shook my hand. "Please have a seat. How can I help you?"

"Have you heard about Doron White?" I settled into a scarred wooden chair.

"Oh yes." He perched on the edge of his desk.

"I talked to Inspector Krisbaum at some length last night—or rather, this morning. I've just given Inspector Kelly a statement outlining everything I did yesterday evening and last night." It took an effort of will not to fidget at the memory. Important to look calm. Trustworthy. "I was nowhere near the financial district last night, Lieutenant. That's in my statement."

"I'm glad to hear it." The merest hint of sarcasm. "But what exactly . . . ?"

"Since I've already given my statement—since there's no way I can misuse the information—I'd really like to know the results of the autopsy. If I could talk to the medical examiner for a few minutes . . . ?"

Surgelato watched me, his face as blank as a baboon's. If I hadn't had a hell of a time cross-examining him in the law-school murders trial, I might have made the mistake of thinking him stupid.

"Why?"

"I worked with Doron for six years. He did more for me—for my career—than anyone."

"I hear he fired you."

Certainly not stupid. "Day before yesterday"—I tried to keep it matter-of-fact—"I made a fool of myself at a press conference."

Surgelato hunched forward. "So he fired you? For one mistake after six years?"

"He wanted me to give up my criminal practice—it was largely pro bono. The Crosetti case certainly was."

I hated baring the guts and gristle of my problem with Doron. But the lieutenant sat there, waiting for more.

If I handled it correctly . . . "I refused to withdraw from the case. Then I got carried away at the deputy DA's press conference." I glanced into the main room.

Inspector Kelly was still typing. "White, Sayres and Speck is a very conservative firm, Lieutenant."

"White had a right to fire you, that what you're saying?"

"More than that. I didn't blame him. I wasn't angry." Doron couldn't contradict me. And I'd hidden it from my colleagues, trying to save face.

"Doron White died in my office. I just want to find out why. How." The unvarnished truth. "It's hell waiting for details when it's someone you know."

Surgelato shook his head. "I'm sorry. You'll have to wait a little longer."

"Why?" I could control my fidgeting; keep temper out of my voice. But I felt myself redden. Damn his hairy hide.

"No specific reason, Ms. Di Palma."

"I've cooperated in every conceivable—"

"It's your duty to cooperate." He stood, stretching slightly; took his time walking behind his desk and sitting in the chair. "Let me put it this way. I may not have a reason right now. But I may not have all the facts. And I'm tired, I haven't had lunch—maybe something's getting by me. Maybe later I *will* think of a reason." A broad Italian shrug. "It's safer to preserve my options. As a lawyer, I'm sure you understand."

Again I looked out into the common room. Good timing: Kelly was just pulling the sheet out of his typewriter.

"I've been doing my damnedest not to behave 'as a lawyer,' Lieutenant!" A lot of indignation, some of it real. "I didn't have to put myself through this. I didn't have to talk to your men last night. I didn't have to come here and dictate a statement."

He looked startled. "And I commend you for doing so. I meant no criticism of lawyers—"

"Didn't you?" I leaped to my feet. "You won't do any favors for a lawyer because lawyers never do any favors for you. That's what you mean, isn't it?"

He squinted up at me.

I gestured at the door. "Inspector Kelly just finished typing my statement. He expects me to come out and sign it. What if I pulled this crap on him? Got on my high horse about how I might think of some reason—*later on!*—for not cooperating now? Wouldn't you think it was bull-shit coming from *me*—coming from a lawyer?"

The corner of his mouth twitched; I didn't know him well enough to know if it was ire or amusement.

But apparently he understood: Krishaum wanted the statement. I didn't have to sign it.

No use leaving the hardball on the table.

"I'm sorry, Lieutenant—I'm upset. Things haven't been going well— and Doron . . . I let him down after a six-year association. I'd just like to know—from the lips of a doctor—that it was more than stress—"

"Ms. Di Palma"—he raised both hands—"enough. I hope I'm wrong, but through all the verbiage, I think I'm hearing a threat."

So much for the velvet glove.

He rose, planting his palms on his desktop. "Tell you what we'll do—I don't want to jump to conclusions. And I certainly meant no aspersions on your profession." Another twitch of the mouth. "So why don't you oblige Inspector Kelly right now and sign the statement, and I'll give the matter some more thought. Stop back on your way out, and I'll have a final answer for you."

Quo before *quid.* Definitely smarter than he looked.

25

Dr. Stiglitz waited for me behind the counter in the coroner's office. I looked at him and felt a shock of worry. Why Stiglitz? There were a dozen other qualified medical examiners in the office. Had Homicide specifically requested Stiglitz?

Two days ago, Stiglitz had autopsied Dan Crosetti. This morning he'd done Doron White. Was Homicide looking for a link between the two men?

I could think of only one: Me.

Stiglitz shook my hand, looking a little uncomfortable. "Miss Di Palma, how are you? Uh, Inspector Kelly phoned down. If you'd like to come on back to my office?"

"Thank you." I followed him through the business office. Jesus, here I was again.

Stiglitz was solicitous. He took my arm and settled me into his own padded vinyl chair.

"Would you like some coffee or a soda?" He bent

over me, losing a few pens from his shirt pocket. He smelled of disinfectant.

"No thanks. Can you tell me about Doron White?"

He nodded, dropping into the chair I'd occupied yesterday afternoon. "Yes. We're, uh, releasing the body to the mortuary this afternoon. To his wife."

Did he think I'd come as a representative of the family? "No; I mean, what killed him?"

He twitched his nose, tapped his fingers on his knee. Stalling? What the hell was the problem?

"Well, without getting technical, a heart attack. Incapacitating already damaged valves." He shook his head. "I don't think Mr. White would have lived very much longer, judging from his medical records. But I also think this particular attack may have been brought on by what was happening to him at the time."

"They told me he was 'roughed up.' What exactly does that mean?"

"Well"—Stiglitz frowned—"I'm a little hamstrung here because I can't discuss evidence from the crime scene—"

"From my office."

"Yes. In this case, the crime-scene evidence tells us several things about the sequence of events." He leaned toward me, warming to his subject. "We can go a long way toward reconstructing the scenario from the fiber and tissue evidence in your office."

"Yes?"

"But you see I've only been authorized to discuss the autopsy report." He shrugged. "So I can place the medical data before you, but I can't interpret it for you in terms of explaining what we think happened."

"That's all right." I knew the layout of my office; I

could reconstruct my own damn scenario. "Whatever you can tell me."

Stiglitz pulled one of the pens out of his pocket and reached past me for a sheet of paper. I followed his movement and saw an eight-by-ten glossy of maggot-riddled flesh. Stiglitz pushed it out of the way as he cleared a space on the desk.

He drew two rude outlines of a human body. He labeled one "front" and one "back." On the latter he drew a few X's, mostly on the left side of the body, on the back and hips. One X decorated the back of the head.

"Sharp, hard hits," he explained. "Very little discoloration or bruising of the skin because the heart stopped beating almost immediately thereafter, but we can tell from various indicators in the dermis that sharp contacts occurred."

On the diagram labeled "front" he penned five O's, one on the right side of the chest, three on the right shoulder, and one on the right side of the face.

"Also points of contact, but less sharp. Let us say, contact which would have reddened the dermis for a short period, but resulted in negligible bruising, if any."

"Slaps? Punches?"

"Possibly. Certainly not by a Spinks or a Tyson." He smiled. Then became flustered. "Pardon me. I realize it's not a joking matter."

"The X's, they'd have left marks?"

He nodded, still looking embarrassed.

It didn't take much of a genius to "reconstruct a scenario." Doron White had been pummeled, albeit not viciously, by a left-handed person (which I hoped Inspector Krisbaum had noticed I am not). Then he'd fallen or been pushed against a piece of furniture with many sharp corners.

I visualized my office. Not my desk—it wouldn't have left so many marks. It had to be the hardwood chair, with its zigzag arms and angled back, catching White in the ribs and the hips, then sliding under him as he fell, striking his head.

The chair must have been behind Doron and to his left. Which meant he'd been standing a few feet from my desk, facing it. Talking to someone seated there? (No wonder I was Krisbaum's favorite suspect, left-handed or not. Who was more likely to sit at my desk than me?)

But why would a person sitting at my desk get up and begin punching Doron?

Had Doron surprised someone who wasn't supposed to be there? Someone searching through my drawers?

Someone who rose when White entered the office; who started out when White came forward; who got as far as the chair before meeting White face to face?

Someone who offered blows rather than an explanation?

"Miss Di Palma?" Stiglitz sounded worried.

I continued to stare at his drawings.

"Let me get you some water, shall I?"

Bless his heart, he was worried about me.

"No, I'm okay. Did Doron have a chance to take a heart pill?"

"They were still in his pocket, I'm afraid."

I looked up from the drawings. "Doron used to reach for those pills reflexively." Poor son of a bitch; a lot of good the habit had done him. "The least little upset and he pulled them out of his pocket. If they weren't in his hand—" I could visualize Doron's manicured hand so clearly; its white-knuckled grip on the amber plastic. "The whole thing must have happened too fast for Doron to think about it."

Stiglitz smoothed a cowlick in his hair. "Interesting. Certainly a possibility."

"Did you find anything else? Fibers or hairs or anything in his hands or under his nails?"

"I was told to share only my gross visual observations."

"I'm not asking for the laboratory identification. Just if something was there and what it looked like."

He pondered this. "I suppose that's okay. We did find some fibers on the right hand."

White reaching out to his attacker as he fell? Grabbing a handful of clothing to keep from going down?

"What kind of fibers?"

Stiglitz shook his head. "That's laboratory information."

"What color?"

"Light." He made a tsking sound. "You know, I think that's really about all I can tell you."

Just as well. It was about all I could stand to hear

26

I LEFT THE coroner's office and found myself behind the Hall of Justice. I walked past a wasteland of parking lot, past dozens of police and county cars. I was nearing the front of the building when I heard a man hail me.

"Ms. Di Palma. Whew. Glad I caught you!"

I turned my back on the ugliest sculpture in the city, twenty-five feet of struts and buckled rods. "Do you need something else?"

Inspector Kelly's smooth, almost boyish face looked splotched and damp.

"If I could just ask a few more questions?" More puffing—didn't cops have fitness standards? "We have some fingerprint information. If you could come back up for a minute?"

I glanced at the dreary six-story box. I'd argued in its courts, visited its morgue, bailed clients out of its jails. Now my confrontation with Surgelato left a bad taste in my mouth. "Ask me here. I'm not going back in."

"But it'll only—" His lips pinched into a pruny oval. I must have looked as stubborn as I felt. "Okay. You want to sit?" He took a step toward wide alabaster planters of impatiens that hugged the building.

"No. Just get on with it."

I could hear foot traffic behind me, on the sidewalk beyond the sculpture. Not much of it; this wasn't a walker's part of town. A mile from the civic center, two miles from the financial district, it was a place to get on or off the freeway, a place to get booked or bailed out.

Kelly glanced at the planters, shaking his head as if there were no end to the eccentricity he must tolerate. "Do you know a Henry Di Palma, Junior?"

Hal. I felt like someone cut my strings.

Kelly's reflexes were fast; he grabbed my shoulders. "Is Hal okay? He hasn't been—"

"No. I don't know. You all right? Can you stand?"

"Why are you asking about Hal?"

"The fingerprint computer." He maneuvered me toward the knee-high planter. "It matched a set of prints in your office."

I could feel cold stone through my pant legs. I sat, putting both hands on dirt-dimmed veins of alabaster.

Kelly sat beside me. Behind him, impatiens exploded with red and white blooms. "Obviously you know Henry Di Palma. Is he a relative?"

"Henry, Junior—Hal. Our fathers are second cousins. We grew up—" Not together, definitely not together. "In the same town. I'm not sure about the degree, but we're cousins."

Kelly looked a little disappointed. "So he's been to your office lately?"

Been to my office? Hal acted like the place was a sewer. "Where did you find prints?"

"Desk. Door."

Three visits to my office in three years. The last of them (that I knew of) was nine months ago. The infamous Christmas party. Even if Hal had touched the desk or the door, the prints wouldn't have survived nine months of cleaning.

"Yes," I heard myself lie. "Hal came to my office one night. Several days ago."

"Days ago?" Kelly shook his head. "We had some nice clear prints—unsmudged. You sure it was that long ago?"

I traced an H on the stone ledge. No use lying about something that could be checked. "Hal had an attack of some kind, probably a stroke, eleven days ago."

Again Kelly looked disappointed. Pulled a little notebook from his vest pocket. "Okay. Just for the purpose of checking, where can we find him?"

Doron White hit repeatedly, but weakly, on the right side of his body. Hal was partially paralyzed on the right side. He would hit with his left. Hit weakly because he was right-handed. Because he was sick.

"Miss Di Palma?"

But why? Why would he hit Doron? What rational reason—

I bit my lip, trying to stay focused, to sift the facts and spot the issues. But I could feel my legal training collapse like flimsy scaffolding.

Why should Hal even go to my office? Why not look for me at home? He wasn't thinking clearly. Maybe he was— maybe he'd attacked Doron White because he was—

Kelly gasped with surprise. "Miss Di Palma! What's wrong?"

I could feel the muscles in my face twist, feel the choking surge of tears and mucus. I remembered the look on Hal's face the last time I'd seen him; I felt like I was turning inside out.

I pushed Kelly away when he tried to pat me. Pushed away the handkerchief he offered.

What the hell did I care how I looked? Hal was irrational. Hal was crazy. Nothing would ever be the same.

27

I soaked in my bath, an untouched glass of Stoli beside me on the tile.

I let the water slosh and I listened to afternoon sounds in my apartment. I'd lived here four years and couldn't remember ever sitting home in the afternoon before. I worked Saturdays, and there were usually loose ends to tie up Sunday. When I got home Sunday afternoon, it was errands. A lot of them I trusted to others: housework, groceries, runs to the cleaner. But no one else could keep my wardrobe current. No one else could sit through the thinning and straightening that kept my hair tame and tidy.

I reached for the Stoli, noticing the ghost of a rainbow where the ice had melted. I'd certainly have time now to become familiar with afternoon sounds. I could hear the tick of my alarm clock, the whistle of wind through treetops, a distant cackle of laughter on the links. Now and then my answering machine offered a

precise invitation to leave a message, followed by the
question or comment of someone I didn't know or didn't
care about, a reporter or a former colleague. My brain
shortened one message into singsong tinnitus: "Susan
Yen, again. Nine eight nine, ten ten."

I put the drink down, still untasted. There was no
getting away from the truth.

Hal had been to my office. And his capacity to injure
exactly matched Doron's wounds.

I'd have to marshall medical records and set up psy-
chiatric tests to keep Hal out of jail. If he didn't want
my help, I'd have to declare him incompetent. Become
his conservator.

I pressed wet fists into my eyes.

I could get Hal acquitted of involuntary manslaughter. But the state would move to place him under psy-
chiatric restraint—Atascadero, most likely.

Hal would never forgive my part in shutting him away.
And I wouldn't be able to live with it.

I sank deeper into the bath. Water purled over the
rim of enamel, and I remembered the lapping of Dan
Crosetti's bath water.

What the hell was I doing in the tub anyway? I hadn't
soaked in a tub in years. Was I telling myself I'd ex-
hausted my inner resources, just like Danny?

I blinked water out of my eyes. Nestled in my glass
soap dish was the razor I used on my legs. It was a
lovely curve of chrome, as Art Deco as the turquoise-
and-black tile behind it.

In the steam of scented water and the chill of sobri-
ety, I found that I could think abstractly about Danny's
suicide. Strip it of ugliness.

It was a very Roman way to go. The death of a de-
feated soldier.

And Danny had been a soldier, in his way. He'd given more to his cause than seventies "patriots" had squandered on hawkish generals. He'd fought for twenty-odd years—longer than any war veteran. Robbed of mobility, behind barred windows, he'd remained in the trenches. And there had been no recent upsurge of sentimentality to buoy him—no *Platoon* or *Full Metal Jacket* to foster empathy, no politicians apologizing to veterans of the war at home.

I picked up my stylish little shaver.

Without Hal, life would be like this every day. A bottle of vodka, an acid bath of remorse.

I turned the razor head. The blade dropped out, landing on a cloud of oily bubbles.

I remembered Hal as I'd last seen him, shuffling across a shined wood floor, one arm tucked to his side like a broken wing. I remembered his face, slack on one side, a bitter scowl on the other. And his eyes—confused, resentful, ashamed.

I picked up the sliver of stainless steel.

I told myself I was just experimenting—a homage to Dan Crosetti. I touched the razor to my wrist and felt a sudden prick of possibility. A door of escape opening.

I sat like that a long time, pressing the razor in a little deeper, a little deeper.

When the water got cold, when the room got dark, I dropped the razor into my tumbler of Stoli. I looked closely at my wrist and saw that I'd broken the skin, but hadn't drawn blood.

I stood shakily, one hand on the slick tile. My flesh rose in goose bumps, and I doubled over, head swimming.

I took a deep breath and straightened again. I reached

for a towel and saw him framed in the doorway like an apparition.

Just standing there.

"Hal."

His head jerked as if I'd slapped him. In the fading light, I fancied that the right side of his face matched the left. When his lip trembled, it trembled on both sides. His wince was equally, painfully pronounced on each side.

He pointed to my wrist. "I thought you were going to do it," he whispered.

He moved quickly across the room. Quickly enough to catch me.

28

I WAS ON the tile floor, looking up at Sandy.

His face was white with worry. He was covering me in towels. "Sweetheart? Are you okay?"

"Hal. Hal was—" I wrapped my arms around Sandy. Oh God, what if Hal *wasn't*? "Were you standing in the doorway? Did you say—"

"Yes." He eased me back, looking at me, looking scared. "You called me Hal. Did you think—?"

I gripped Sandy until I had no tears left.

It was pitch black in the room by the time I sat back to mop my face.

Sandy rose to one knee, reaching for the light switch.

"No," I begged. "Don't."

He left the light off, sighing deeply. "I just heard about Doron White." His voice was hushed. He'd worked for Doron longer, if less closely, than I had. "Catch me up. Can you?"

"I talked to the medical examiner," I told him wearily. "Doron was hit on the right side. Punches or slaps—nothing heavy. He fell. I'm fairly sure he fell against my wood chair, the postmodern with all the jags and points. Hit his back and left hip. Probably someone at the desk got up and tried to get past him. Surprised him. Doron didn't have his pills in his hand."

We sat in the dark room, listening to a drip of water from faucet to tub, inhaling the damp perfume of bath oil.

Sandy rose slowly, brushing his fingertips down my arm until he found my hand. He wrapped his fingers around mine and pulled me to my feet. My towels fell away, but it was too dark for me to care. I let him put his arm around me and walk me into the bedroom.

My answering machine glowed with red and green lights, announcing the time, 6:54, and the number of messages, 7. Outside the window, streetlamps lit a stand of eucalyptus and made fluttering shadows on my wall. My bed was still unmade and the comforter still dragged, as if it had been one day, and not eleven, since I'd found Hal on the carpet.

I pulled a robe out of my closet and threaded my arms into the sleeves. My skin felt bloodlessly cold.

Sandy turned on a tiny reading lamp, twisting the gooseneck so that it lit a far corner of wainscot.

He pulled the trailing comforter back onto the bed and sat heavily atop it, running both hands over the back of his head.

"We're going to solve this thing, Laura. Me and you. We're going to figure this thing out."

I fumbled with the tie on my robe.

He looked up at me. He looked haggard and sad. "You're the smartest lady I know. I need you working on this with me. I need you thinking. Not—" he extended his hand—"not falling apart on me. Not playing with razors."

"Hal was at the office last night, Sandy." I took the hand he offered. "They found his prints on my desk and on the door."

A brief silence while he stared at our linking hands. "He'd have no reason on God's earth to hurt Doron."

"He might not—" I tried to ease my hand out of his. "He might not need—"

Sandy held fast. "Might not need a reason? Laura? Look at me, will you?"

I looked. His eyes were heavy-lidded and bright.

"You're afraid Hal's nuts. You're thinking his brains got so scrambled by that bullet in Vietnam . . . that maybe he's one of these walking time bombs you hear about on television. Maybe he was on the edge all these years, barely keeping it together. You're thinking back on things he did that might have been early signs. And you're thinking that whatever went wrong with him this time, whatever screwed up the right side of his body, it must have made the craziness worse."

I couldn't bring myself to nod.

"Now I'm going to tell you what I think." A mirthless smile. "I've met your family. Maybe it's because of them or maybe it's some inborn thing. But I think Hal would have been a bad-tempered, selfish asshole, bullet or not."

I drew back, trying to jerk my hand out of his.

But he hung on. "I won't pretend I like Hal. I won't pretend it's fine by me if he gives you three years of constant shit." A ripple of jaw muscles. "I met you, you were confident and self-assured. Three years of Hal tearing you down, and you're in the fucking bathtub with a razor on your wrist."

"That's got nothing to do with Hal tearing me down."

"Like hell."

"I'm not such a delicate flower, Sandy." I succeeded in pulling my hand away. "It doesn't matter what Hal *says*. Don't you see the way he—" The way he looks at me. "It's not me Hal attacks. It's affluence. He feels guilty about it."

I thought of Dan Crosetti's apartment—a few hours there had tarnished my enjoyment of this modest luxury. How would years of rootless poverty change my perception?

"Christ." Sandy slumped, hands on his knees. "I didn't mean to open up *that* can of worms. The point is, I've got no particular love for Hal—and about as much respect for him as you could fit into an acorn. And I'm telling you"—he paused for effect—"the guy is not crazy! He's got a lousy disposition, but he's not crazy!"

"The stroke, or whatever it was—"

"Made him weak and confused. But he got better. He got better enough to leave the damn hospital. He got better enough to come back to San Francisco—to watch the goddamn television news, to go to a bar and call you up. Jesus God, Laura! His message to you— did he sound crazy? Did he sound mixed-up even?"

"Sad."

Sandy stood listlessly. "Yeah, sad."

"But you don't think he punched Doron?"

"No." He shook his head positively. "He'd have no reason. It was somebody snooping around your office. I don't know what the hell for, but it must have to do with Crosetti and Lefevre. It's the only thing you're into that anybody would care about."

Crosetti and Lefevre. "Every time I try to think about them or do something constructive in the case—"

"Hal—I know." He stooped so that we were practically nose to nose. "Listen, Laura, they unsealed your office as of right before I came over here. I came to pick you up. I want you to go there with me. I want to brainstorm with you." He looked into my eyes as if checking pupil dilation. "It's the best thing you could do for Hal. If you're up to it."

I felt chilled and nauseous and dizzy. "Give me five minutes to dress."

29

We weren't alone in the offices of White, Sayres & Speck. In fact, all but two of the associates were working, and the nighttime word processors were there in force. Doron White might have been the first name on the letterhead, but he was probably the most expendable lawyer in the firm.

People were exaggeratedly polite about my return. I realized it might be possible to slip back into the job from which Doron White had fired me. White's partners would find it easier than parceling my work among already-overworked associates—and certainly easier than taking it on themselves. And they wouldn't have to worry about my stealing away bank clients. If I stopped rocking the boat, they might pretend nothing had happened. Even vote me into their ranks next March.

But I might as well spit on Doron's grave.

I closed my office door and leaned against it, watching Sandy prowl and sniff and riffle. Except for the skewed placement of chairs and desk, the office looked much as usual.

Sandy sat in the chair behind the desk and opened the top drawer. "So what the hell could you have that somebody else would want?"

I chose to ignore the existential implications of the question. "A bunch of boring pleadings in there—nobody would want those."

I dragged the leather chairs back to where they had been, and returned the postmodern hardwood to where it belonged. "Belonged"—I supposed that was for the next occupant of this office to determine.

"I was at Dan Crosetti's apartment twice. I could have taken something either time."

"The first visit—when you found Crosetti in the bathtub?" Sandy let a desk drawer roll shut, opened the next one. "Who knew about it?"

"That day, the authorities: paramedics, cops, FBI, deputy DA." And after my press conference, anyone within range of broadcast signals. "Next morning it was on the news."

Sandy looked up at me, considering. "On the news."

"But Danny was dying. I wouldn't look through his things while he was—" I sat heavily in the hardwood chair, careful to keep my hands off its zigzag arms. I'd never forget the coroner's reference to tissue evidence.

Sand-colored hair spilled over Sandy's forehead as he slammed the second drawer. "He could have given you something to keep for him. You were his lawyer. You were there when he died."

"Except that—"

"Except nothing. The news didn't give the gory details. If anything, it left the impression Crosetti died slowly in your— sorry." He slouched back in the chair.

"But Crosetti could have entrusted something to you. I mean, as far as anyone else knows. Right?"

I rubbed my neck. "I suppose so."

"Then yesterday afternoon, you go back to Danny's. You had to sign in, right? So your name was on the coroner's seal—"

"The seal was coming down that evening. The coroner said so." We'd been through this over pasta the night before. It was starting to feel like a drill, like witness preparation.

"And you didn't see anything that set off bells."

"No. His papers were in neat piles—already sorted through. Nothing incriminating. Not even suggestive— not to me, anyway."

"But that night someone comes to your office. Probably sits here and does what I'm doing now—pokes through your desk. Doron comes in, and Person X stands up. X wants to get out of here, but he has to push Doron around to get past him." He rubbed his knuckles over his chin. "That the sequence as you see it?"

"Yes."

"Well"—he sat forward, elbows on the blotter—"I'm not sure what the hell the chronology means. But my gut feeling says someone's looking for something of Crosetti's. Something they think he gave you or you took."

"Why search my office? Why not my apartment?"

"Would you know if your apartment was searched? Could you tell if it was done carefully? If you weren't looking for signs?"

"You're the detective. Could I?"

"Nope. Not if it was done with finesse." In rapid

succession, he opened and closed each of the remaining desk drawers.

Then he stood slowly, massaging his chest where he'd taken the bullets. "Have a look—make sure everything's here that should be. Make sure this whole thing isn't about stealing Exalted American Bank's files."

My throat burned for a drink; things were getting too focused. I'd been tempted to set up a wet bar in the cabinet by the bookcase. It was something Doron White could have done—it would have made him seem hospitable and distinguished. But I'd been afraid of looking hard and trampy.

"You okay, sweetheart?"

"I could use—" I thought of the tumbler of vodka beside my bathtub. "Coffee, I guess."

"Perfect." He tucked his shirt more tidily into his trousers, impatiently shrugging his jacket into place. Long and lean, he'd have looked terrific in his suit if he hadn't worn it with obvious annoyance. "I need to talk to the secretaries. Coffee's a good cover."

Something about Sandy—a seductive voice and "Shucks, ma'am" manners—won him a lot of information, especially "below stairs."

On his way out; he stopped and squatted beside my chair. He slipped a long hand behind my neck and leaned forward, briefly pressing his lips to mine. He might as well have kissed a statue.

He averted his eyes. Behind him, a wall of glass framed a night scene of city lights, of tangled traffic and office windows. Sandy walked quickly and stiffly out of the room.

I stood, moving listlessly to the chair behind the desk. I began with the top left drawer. Xeroxed cases. I went through them, one by one; went on to the next drawer.

Files. I went through them. Went through more drawers, more files. Hundreds of hours of strategy; of carefully conceived and researched arguments; phrases chosen to persuade the judge and inflame the opposition. Paper warfare, waged with ferocity and fanfare—over mere collateral.

Slumped in my chair, I remembered Dan Crosetti's files. He'd chosen his battles more carefully; he'd exercised his conscience, not his acumen.

I pressed the heels of my hands to my eyes, feeling the inkling of an idea. I tried to visualize Danny's apartment from the perspective of myself on the floor, sifting through files. I'd looked up, glancing at the walls, and—

I opened my eyes, blinking. There'd been an empty space on the wall where I'd seen a map the day before. If I remembered correctly, a Nuclear Watch map of California, showing routes of trucks carrying nuclear weapons.

Something the FBI might pull down and tuck into a file.

I punched 9 for an outside line, and I phoned the Clearinghouse.

"Clearinghouse. Asimov."

Someone I knew. Good. "This is Laura Di Palma. Are you usually there so late?"

"It's only eight-thirty, and yes"—a verbal sneer—"I usually am."

"Have you been looking through boxes?" I felt a twist of guilt. I'd promised Barbara Nottata I'd send Sandy over to help.

"Yes." He didn't sound happy about it. "Not that I have any right to."

I had yet to meet a cop who took the Fourth Amendment so seriously. "Your motives are pure."

"Did you want something?"

"I assume you haven't found anything?"

"No. I've got maybe six, eight boxes left."

"What can you tell me about Nuclear Watch?"

"They've been around quite a while. They put out flyers on what the latest trucks look like, the ones carrying nuclear weapons or nuclear waste. They have spotters up and down the state—kind of like birdwatchers—counting trucks and mapping routes."

"What do they do with the information?"

His voice warmed. "Pretty smart stuff. They work up maps and make them available to other organizations—CalPIRG, for instance—that talk to people living along the routes. Quite a few communities have passed ordinances barring the trucking from county throughways—Nuclear Free Zones. They also show up at Department of Highways hearings. They help the Ploughshares people figure out where to lay their bodies. They publish maps and stats in *Nuclear Times*. And they're kind of a bridge between the Teach Peace people and the militant anarchist types."

"The information they pass out, is any of it classified?"

"Oh yeah. The government keeps changing the fucking trucks. They don't want to be pissing around with local ordinances and old WILPF ladies lying in the road."

"Where does Nuclear Watch get its information?"

A pause. "Hell if I know."

"Are you going to be there awhile?"

"Yeah."

"I'll come by in about an hour."

"I'll stay anyway." He hung up.

Sandy stepped back into the room, rubbing his jaw thoughtfully. "Want to hear something funny?"

I replaced the receiver. "What?"

"The ladies in word processing didn't see anybody but lawyers last night, and the lawyers didn't see anybody but word processors."

He plunked his long body into one of the chairs. "So maybe it's got nothing to do with Crosetti, after all. Maybe it was a beef between Doron and Jerry, or Doron and Tish."

"Tish is an ass kisser. Jerry is a wimp."

A half smile, gone as soon as it appeared. "Well, there must have been awhile there when nobody was paying attention. Or how the hell did Hal come and go?"

No one would mistake Hal for a lawyer.

Sandy looked startled. "I forgot the coffee." Then irritated. "What's the matter with me, anyway? I'm so damn scattered."

I thought of Hal sitting at my desk. I put my hands on the blotter and tried to absorb some lingering sense of his presence.

"You look wrung-out, sweetheart. Want to call it a night?"

"We need to go to the Clearinghouse. Barbara Nottata—"

"Who?"

"A friend of Danny's. She looked around the Clearinghouse and found Danny's FBI file in a box no one ever opens. She's new in town, didn't know Danny that well, so I had her ask Keith Asimov—do you know who—"

"Yuh. Punky-looking guy."

"He's been going through every box in the place. I was just talking to him."

I told Sandy about the map missing from Dan Crosetti's wall. Told him what Asimov had said about Nuclear Watch. "Maybe the organization got hold of classified information—maybe Danny did. Maybe that's what Danny's supposed to have given me. The reason my office was searched."

Sandy stretched his long legs, massaging his knees. "The only people interested in that kind of stuff are people who could get themselves a warrant to look for it."

I folded my arms over my blotter and let my head rest there.

Sandy's voice was gentle. "Say the FBI thought Crosetti had classified information. They'd be into those file boxes like cockroaches. And if they thought Crosetti gave you something top secret before he died, you'd have white shirts all over you."

"I suppose," I mumbled into my arms.

"The FBI's just about the most paranoid, fucked-up bunch of assholes in the world, but I'll tell you one thing—they're not so stupid they'd push around an important lawyer like Doron White."

"All right! It was just an idea."

He tsked. "We're scattered," he repeated. "We need to be a little more organized in our thinking. Laura? Would you look at me, please?"

I obliged him.

"Number one: Somebody killed John Lefevre."

"And number two: Dan Crosetti is arrested."

Sandy frowned. "Did Crosetti ever tell you how he found out about Lefevre? You with me? How he found out Lefevre was FBI?"

"No."

A moment of silence. It might as well have been written in neon: *And you call yourself a lawyer?*

"What *did* you talk about?"

"Right after his arrest, we talked about his medical condition."

"His medical—" Sandy looked perplexed. "Why?"

"Because that's what I needed to know to force an immediate bail hearing. I figured if I got him out of there, we could sweat the details later."

"So what about later?"

I was too weary to feel ashamed, and it was a damn good thing. "I didn't see him again for a week. I was at the hospital with Hal, and—Danny and I were just starting to talk facts when I got the call that Hal was gone."

"And when you went to Crosetti's apartment—" His face was pinched. "Don't get mad, now—but did he actually *say* he didn't kill Lefevre? Right out?"

"He didn't have to say so. It was implicit in everything he— Look, I walked out of Danny's apartment as sure as a person can be that Lefevre's killer was still at large." I took a deep breath. "And morally responsible for Danny's suicide."

Sandy frowned, sweeping a straggle of hair off his forehead. "I'm just saying Crosetti had the means and he had the motive—"

"Everyone at the Clearinghouse had the same motive!"

"No—we're talking about betrayal. And what I hear is, Crosetti was close to Lefevre. That pushes the knife in deeper."

A name formed itself on my lips. "Keith Asimov."

Sandy nodded slowly. "Yuh. I suppose a friend of Crosetti's might take it pretty damn personally."

"But he wouldn't stand by and let Danny take the blame."

"Well—it'd be nice to think Crosetti had better friends than that." His lips curled cynically. "But if Lefevre's any example, Crosetti didn't exactly choose his comrades wisely."

I remembered the stirring of distrust I'd rejected that morning. "You're straight with me, aren't you, Sandy?"

"What's that mean?"

"What you told me about John Lefevre living in the Haight? Taking drugs?" Barbara Nottata's observation rankled.

"Yeah?"

"Wouldn't the FBI have known that?"

"One presumes. What's your drift, Laura?"

"Why did the FBI take Lefevre back? Give him a new assignment?"

"I happen to have a theory about that. But I'd rather know why you— No." He scowled. "One thing at a time. I think the white shirts had their doubts about Lefevre—taking time off, hanging around with old flower children. My guess is they wanted to warehouse him for a while. Find out exactly what was shaking with him." He brushed some graphite off the leather chair arm. "They wanted to put him someplace he might find out good stuff—no use wasting taxpayers' money—but also someplace he couldn't fuck up an existing operation. So they stuck him in with a bunch of has-been pacifists."

"You didn't mention this theory before."

His jaw muscles rippled. "And you didn't mention thinking I'm a liar."

30

IT WAS A ten-minute ride to the Clearinghouse, through the financial district and across Market, through the Mission district with its smell of refried beans and atmosphere of church and family, and into the Noe Valley with its thriving little nightclubs and graceful Victorians. I closed my burning eyes and rested my head on the overstuffed seat of Sandy's Buick. We didn't speak.

When we got to Twenty-fourth, Sandy started looking for a parking place. We circled another ten minutes, and I watched gay couples saunter and hug and laugh and jostle their way into bars and restaurants. We found a spot off Castro. Sandy unlocked the trunk, looked quickly around, and pulled a revolver out of a small case. He unbuttoned his jacket and fastened the gun to his belt. He slammed the trunk and turned to me, looking grim, almost defiant. He didn't say anything and I didn't either. We walked the five blocks to the Clearinghouse.

It was one of many places on Twenty-fourth that was still lighted and open to the public. Across the street, couples lined up outside a tiny restaurant. A knot of people huddled in front of a bookstore.

Through lowered matchstick blinds, I could see Keith Asimov moving around the Clearinghouse. I felt Sandy's arm slide around my shoulders.

I broke the silence we'd erected between us. "It doesn't even rise to the level of a guess, Sandy."

"I know."

"You're not going to pull the gun?"

"Give me some credit."

He reached out and opened the Clearinghouse door.

Asimov wheeled around. He looked through me. "The detective," he said to Sandy.

There's a kind of man who will always talk to another man—any other man—in preference to a woman. Apparently Asimov was one of them.

I walked past the two front desks and examined the wall of file boxes dividing the room. No evidence of boxes displaced or papers rummaged.

Behind me, Sandy said, "Where did Crosetti keep his rifle?"

I turned in time to see Asimov shrug. His hair was disheveled, his skin smudged. Maybe he had been searching.

"Nobody ever proved to me that he had one," Asimov said.

A man's head crested the boxes—someone rising from a crouch or a squat. Lank blond hair over thin cheeks, oatmeal skin: Mark Bresenzcy, the young lawyer.

"Hi." He smiled at me, nodded politely to Sandy, then bent in a fit of sneezing.

Ignoring him, I told Asimov, "Danny admitted to me—"

But Asimov cut me off. "I knew Danny a hell of a lot better than you did. If he had a rifle—"

"No doubt about it," Sandy drawled.

"Yeah, well, I never saw or heard anything to prove it."

Bresenzcy, recovered from his sneezes, interjected, "He wouldn't have kept it here."

"Because he never fucking owned one!" Asimov insisted.

Bresenzcy stepped out from behind the file-box wall. He shook his head, but he didn't appear angry.

I looked at Asimov's red face. Sandy was wrong: this was a man who stood by his friends.

Reluctantly I persisted. "Danny admitted he bought the rifle. He told me he was ashamed to say so in front of you."

Asimov's face twisted as if I'd lashed him.

Sandy's voice was harsh. "So which one of you macho revolutionaries found Crosetti's rifle? Which one of you blew away the fuzz?"

The getting of information was Sandy's bailiwick. I took an effacing step backward. But I couldn't help wondering how much of Sandy's scorn was real.

Sandy stopped slouching; grew taller and more imposing. "It's pretty obvious, isn't it? We keep hearing all this crap about the great Dan Crosetti—how you all revered and admired the man." He made a "big deal" gesture. "But mostly you were jealous of Lefevre—the way he swapped poetry with Crosetti, practically became his blood brother in one fucking month"—he stepped closer to Asimov—"when you'd been carrying

Crosetti's crutches low long? How long were you Crosetti's errand boy?''

''You're an ignorant, offensive son of a bitch,'' Asimov said quietly.

''Well, okay''—with exaggerated, patronizing sarcasm—''since I happen to know anyway. You've been Crosetti's gofer for the last four years. Four years!—and I bet he never showed *you* his poetry.''

Asimov was white-faced, scowling. ''Fuck off.''

Sandy seemed to snap. He lunged forward, grabbing Asimov by the shirt front. ''You want to say that again, pacifist?''

Mark Bresenzcy started toward them, but I motioned him back, motioned him to be quiet. He obeyed immediately; he'd make someone a hell of a good junior associate.

Sandy and Asimov were toe to toe now, with Sandy latched onto and bowed over the shorter man. ''I know a lot about you,'' he whispered. ''You and your ilk. Wouldn't fight in the war where you might have done somebody some good, but you sure didn't think twice about bashing peace officers with rocks and bricks.''

I was getting a little scared. Sandy had been a ''peace officer'' in the late sixties and early seventies. Was this a sample of the era's interrogation techniques?

Asimov scrambled to stay on his feet as Sandy bent him backward. Asimov's arms trembled as if it were all he could do to keep them at his sides.

Bresenzcy started forward, but again I motioned him to stop.

As long as Sandy challenged Asimov's pacifism, he was safe—protected from violence by Asimov's stubbornness. And as long as Asimov remained pacific, Sandy would only taunt and bully.

Still, the spectacle disgusted me. I heard myself beg, "Leave him alone, Sandy."

Instead, Sandy executed a slow shuffle across the room, pushing Asimov backward and bouncing him off fists knotted into his shirt. Sandy's jaw was thrust forward, his lip lifted in a sneer.

I'd never seen Sandy look like that; didn't know what it meant. But I dutifully sidled in front of Bresenzcy, barring him from interfering. As much as I wanted the ugly scene to end, I had to give Sandy some rope.

Sandy backed Asimov into the wall of file boxes. The men were close enough that I could smell their overheated fury. I could feel Bresenzcy stir behind me.

Suddenly Sandy pulled Asimov forward till they were chest to chest. "Tell me something, pacifist. How'd you get out of active duty?" He slammed Asimov back against the boxes. "Flat feet? Allergies?"

He pulled Asimov forward and rammed him back again. The boxes slid and shifted with the impact, raising a cloud of dust.

I never thought I'd see Sandy act like such a pig.

Another slam. "Or were you getting a fucking master's degree someplace?"

"Listen, fucker—" Asimov spoke through teeth so tightly clenched it looked painful. His skin was splotched red, dripping sweat. "I've been arrested six times. There's nothing you can do to me some asshole cop hasn't done already."

Sandy grabbed one of Asimov's hands, pulling it to eye level in spite of Asimov's furious squirming. "Well, you still got your trigger finger—guess you didn't cut it off to get your Four-F. Guess you didn't go in for self-mutilation, like Crosetti."

I heard Bresenzcy gasp. Maybe I did too. Sandy had gone too far.

Apparently Asimov agreed. His free arm came up fast and hard, knocking Sandy away. As Sandy released him, the countermotion threw Asimov backward, off balance.

It was more than the tottering wall of boxes could take. The top rows toppled. Boxes dropped with muffled thuds, corners flattening, lids bouncing, papers spilling. Dust and paper shavings choked the air.

Asimov might have fallen too, but Sandy grabbed him, spinning him 180 degrees, so his back was to the door. Asimov, gasping to recover his equilibrium, flailed his arms, blinking as if he couldn't quite focus.

Sandy hooked his foot behind Asimov's. Pushed. Asimov went down with a bonecracking thud.

Sandy stood over him, glowering. "That was for Doron White, asshole!"

Behind me, Bresenzcy whispered, "Oh, Jesus!"

Asimov scrambled quickly to his feet, jumping aside as what remained of the box wall collapsed. A tidal wave of spilled papers surged toward Sandy.

The distraction lasted only a moment. Then Asimov spat, "You don't give a shit about Dan Crosetti! You just want to do some dove bashing!" He assumed a fighting stance, legs wide, knees bent, fingers curled. "You think I don't recognize you? You think you're the first bastard ever walked in here pissed off because he fought the good fight and I didn't?"

Sandy was much whiter than he should have been, given his exertion. His lips were pinched into a downward arc. His brows were lower than I'd ever seen them. Only his flared nostrils showed a blush of color.

Asimov staggered back a half step, then straightened.

"Let me tell you who you're really mad at, asshole!" He stood stiffly, almost militarily. "You're mad at yourself for letting the government use you as fodder. You're mad at yourself for bombing and defoliating a nice little country and killing a bunch of farmers. You're mad at yourself because now everyone knows the war was bullshit, and you were too fucking stupid at the time—"

Sandy lashed out with his open hand—a hard, fast slap that rocked Asimov. That would have knocked him down if he hadn't jerked and shuffled himself back into place.

Ostentatiously, Asimov presented Sandy his other cheek.

"No!" My voice was sharp. No more rope.

Sandy didn't even glance at me. He watched Asimov with a look of blank hatred; he began reaching under his jacket.

I started forward, but I wasn't fast enough. The men came together with the force of clashing rams.

They did a few lurching turns and I tracked them, sidling and gasping like some ringside cheerleader. Finally, they parted long enough for me to squeeze between them.

I faced Sandy, so close to his chest that I could feel the heat waves of hatred. For a moment I was afraid his momentum would crush me against Asimov.

Behind me I heard the tinkle of a bell, but I didn't associate it with the door. My consciousness was bounded by sweating men.

Barbara Nottata's voice cut through the pumping adrenalin. She said, quite calmly, "Laura, can I talk to you?"

A rush of air at my back told me Asimov had moved away.

I glanced over my shoulder at Barbara, but couldn't seem to gear down to respond. I vaguely noticed Bresenzcy leaving through the open door.

I looked up at Sandy. He appeared damp and spent; and I was reminded—to my chagrin—of lying in his arms.

He looked over my head with a lift of the lips I'd never describe as a smile. "Well, well," he murmured. "Would you look at that?"

I turned around.

Keith Asimov was holding a gun.

I felt Sandy's hand on my shoulder. "Mine," he murmured. "I wondered if the son-of-a-bitch was ever going to take it!" He stepped sideways, stepping around me. "So you know how to handle firearms. Thought you might."

Asimov tapped the smallish revolver so that the revolving cylinder swung out. He peered into the chambers. Then he tossed the gun.

I watched it arc across the room, turning a slow, awkward spiral. It landed at Sandy's feet.

Asimov said, "Thank fucking goodness it's empty. You're crazy—way too crazy to carry a loaded gun."

Sandy squatted to retrieve the gun, snapping the cylinder back into place.

And Barbara Nottata observed, "Not crazy, Keith. I think he got just what he wanted from you."

31

BARBARA NOTTATA MOVED to center stage. She interposed herself between me and Keith Asimov. When I could no longer see around her, when I finally looked at her face, she stopped, aware that she'd found the right spot. Then she derailed my train of thought.

"You had a phone call here. From Hal Di Palma."

It was a difficult transition from the fight—from wondering what the hell Sandy had accomplished and whether his real attitudes had surfaced in the process.

Sandy stepped back into line with me, putting his arm around me. Behind Barbara, Asimov stretched his arms, making her look like a pompadoured Kali.

"When did he call?"

"Right before I left. Maybe an hour ago." She unbuttoned her peacoat, revealing the Fair Isles sweater in which I'd seen her earlier. "The message was so unusual I tried calling you several times."

"What did he say?" Why in God's name had he left a message here?

"I'd rather tell you privately."

Sandy's arm tightened around my shoulder. "If he wants to meet you, let me come along," he urged. "You might need help with him."

The possibility of seeing Hal sliced through every other concern. "Does he want to meet me?"

She inclined her head toward the door. "I think the message is private."

I had to push Sandy away to follow her. On my way out, I noticed Asimov backing toward a wall of announcements—*Hiroshima Day Vigil, Nicaraguan Mothers of the Heroes and Martyrs Benefit Dinner, Nuclear Weapons Freeze Walk-a-thon, San Francisco Bay Women's Alliance Hotline*. He was obviously reluctant to remain alone with Sandy.

I joined Barbara outside. She was standing with her back to the matchstick blinds, looking across the street at a restaurant line of cuddling couples. A few yards behind her, window shoppers with turned-up collars priced best-sellers. In the howl of night wind, her moussed hair flattened, making her look plainer and less citified.

With my shoulder, I kept the Clearinghouse door ajar. "What did he say?"

She seemed distracted, blinking into the wind. "He said he'd been to Danny's house. That you should go to Danny's." She caught her lower lip between her teeth, glancing behind me at the door. "He also said, 'Lose Sandy.' "

I took a slow step forward, letting the door close. "Is Hal there now? At Danny's?"

She huddled in her coat. "I don't know."

Away from the shelter of the building, I felt the wind flap my trouser legs, pull my hair back. An aggressively cold autumn, all of a sudden; I knew I should be shivering in my sweater, but I wasn't. "Do you have a car?"

She nodded.

"Will you give me a lift?"

"Right now?" She peered worriedly through the matchsticks.

"Please?" I was counting on her midwestern manners.

She gnawed her lip a brief second. "I'm on the rape-crisis hotline tonight. If someone called and I wasn't there for her—"

"Hal escaped from a stroke center. I'm afraid if I don't find him—" In spite of the wind, I felt hot; I could feel my heart pumping, hear it pounding in my ears. "He's probably been sleeping outside. He could be very sick." And very confused. Why go to my office yesterday? Why call me at a political-action center?

"He didn't say he'd be there." Her tone was more concerned than cautionary; a nurse's tone. "Is that man Sandy?" She squinted at the blinds.

"Yes."

She'd seen Sandy at his worst. She certainly wouldn't question Hal's suggestion that I "lose" him.

"It's just that I made this commitment to the hotline that no matter what happened I'd—"

"Asimov's in there. He can get the phone."

"Can you imagine talking to Keith after you'd been—"

"It won't take long. He can handle it."

"Well . . ." She looked shocked. "If you don't mind me just dropping you off."

She walked quickly past me up Twenty-fourth. I put

my fingers on the doorknob, thinking I should tell Sandy I was going.

But Barbara was clearly in a hurry. And maybe I was afraid I'd find another fight in progress if I opened the door.

I caught up with Barbara, surprised when her car turned out to be a jaunty little Colt, nice and clean, almost new, gleaming under a streetlamp. She unlocked the driver's door and climbed in, moving a stack of papers and a battered briefcase off the passenger seat before unlocking my door for me.

As I climbed in, I looked over my shoulder. Sandy was striding toward us.

I would have waited for him; explained where I was going. But Barbara noticed him and gave a small gasp. Hurriedly she fumbled the keys into the ignition.

As she squealed the car out of its parking place, I rolled down the passenger window and shouted, "Call you later."

I heard Sandy shout something about an idiot—me, presumably.

By the time we were half a block away, Sandy stood in the empty parking place, notebook in hand, jotting something down.

Probably Barbara's license plate number.

32

IN THE FAINT light of a half moon and a distant street-lamp, Barbara Nottata's face looked blank. Only the widely opened eyes betrayed fear. She might act calm and tough, and so might I, but this was no neighbor-hood to frequent after dark.

She looked beyond me out the passenger window. "How are you going to get in?"

Crosetti's front door looked solid and black in the moonlight—no coroner's seal nailed to it. The bars on his windows glinted. Behind them, two panes of glass had been shattered. Newspapers and cigarette butts and crushed paper cups tumbled down the street. Some-where out of sight, a man howled like a wolf.

"The coroner gave me a duplicate of Danny's house key. The seal was due to come down, so nobody needed the key back."

That had been my excuse for keeping it. But my rea-son had to do with Danny. I'd stood on the other side of a door listening to him die. What I had failed to do for him literally and legally I would do symbolically. I would retain access to his life. I would keep the investigation alive—keep the door open.

I reached into my purse and extracted my key ring— car, apartment house, apartment, office building, office suite. And the coroner's duplicate of Danny's key, shiny and sharp-edged. I took a deep breath before opening the car door. The street was deserted, but that didn't make it seem any safer.

I was surprised to hear Barbara's door open, too. She murmured, "You're going to need a ride back."

"Thanks." Heartfelt.

Our car doors slammed in the silence. As we crossed to Danny's door, music suddenly blared from the apartment above, the perky theme of some situation comedy, surrealistically inappropriate to the dreary rows of "temporary" double-deckers. The smell of brine and rancid fat blew down the street.

The howling started again, more silly than scary against the television background. Nevertheless, it was a relief to unlock the door and go inside. And I was glad Barbara had remained.

I clicked on the light. By any measure, it was a depressing room. The bedsheet curtains, the battered furniture, the handicapped-access arrangement, the stacks of police-inspected papers, the posters of slogans and rallying cries—the place had an atmosphere of an uphill—a losing—battle.

"Where do you live, Barbara?"

"Mission district." She looked around the living room, sighing. "We don't have Mexican food where I come from. It's really a treat."

Most neighborhoods in the city were a treat, one way or another. Hunters Point was an exception.

Barbara squatted beside a stack of newsletters, riffling them abstractedly. Then she looked up, her gaze settling on the bare spot of wall that had once sported a Nuclear Watch map.

"Did you come to Danny's very often?" I asked her.

She continued frowning at the blank meter of wall. "Several times, yes."

"There was a map up there, wasn't there?"

"Yes. With bead-head thumbtacks. Different colors. Danny moved them around."

"Nuclear Watch, right?"

She rose from her squat, unbuttoning her peacoat. Upstairs, a television child was being loudly precocious, to the delight of a knee-slapping laugh track. "I don't think so. I think it was the cross-country Peace March—the one that took a year. Danny wanted to go. On crutches, you know, to really make a point."

She was wrong. The map had been of California, clearly labeled Nuclear Watch.

"Why didn't he go?"

She shucked the jacket. "A lot of people were encouraging him because of the publicity, and he really wanted to do it." She shook her head. "But he knew he couldn't. It was just too far, too long—it would have been terribly grueling and painful. He'd have slowed everyone down, and he probably wouldn't have made it to the end anyway. He wasn't twenty anymore."

I sat in Danny's easy chair, uncomfortably aware of its third-hand grime and broken springs. "You were a nurse. Did he talk to you about it?"

She turned her face away as she slipped her jacket over the back of a hard chair. "No. I'm just assuming."

"Ironic." Maybe Danny would be weary and ill in the middle of Missouri now instead of dead in the safety of his hometown.

Barbara sat on the wooden chair, her spine very straight, her knees together, her hands folded.

"Barbara, what you said about Hal—about him saying to come here, to Danny's house?"

She continued sitting straight and still.

"I've already looked through all these papers. So have the police and the FBI. There's nothing here. Besides," I glanced at the barred windows. "Hal couldn't possibly have gotten in since Danny died."

"That's true. The message—"

"Was your way of getting in here. You knew I had a key, didn't you?"

We looked at one another. She looked like what she claimed to be—a middle-class nurse who'd turned to activism to salve her own wounds. A statistically significant percentage of activists must fit that description.

I tried to ignore the poking springs of Danny's chair, the ancient dog smell of it, the ranting and laughing of the television above. I tried to ignore the wrenching conclusion to be drawn from the statement I'd just blurted.

"It didn't occur to me until now. You're really good, Barbara."

Barbara was pale, her brows twisted with worry. She gnawed the inside of her cheek.

"Oh God." I relaxed against the back of Danny's chair. "Hal's not coming. You never talked to him, did you? Why would he even call the Clearinghouse?" My eyes burned, but I was all cried out. "And your reluctance to drive me here was just a show, wasn't it? So I wouldn't feel maneuvered into coming."

Her voice shook a little. "You look awful. Can I do anything?"

"Danny's FBI file wasn't at the Clearinghouse, was it? You got it straight from the source, didn't you?"

She was as still and pale as a statue. Beside her, dust funneled above a table lamp.

"You're an FBI agent, aren't you, Barbara?"

When she didn't answer, I continued, "Danny's files were just bait. They got you into my house so you could look around for whatever you guys are really after."

"No. I just wanted to know you better. To see if I could talk to you."

Upstairs, a commercial promised "relief from the aches and pains of head colds and hay fever!"

"You were assigned to watch John Lefevre. The bureau didn't trust him because of his six-month leave. So it sent him someplace—" how had Sandy described the Clearinghouse?—"someplace innocuous. And they sent you to make sure Lefevre was still a loyal agent."

Barbara's cheeks grew pink; her gaze dropped to her neatly polished nails.

"Only he wasn't, was he? He got close to Dan Crosetti, and he began to admire him and agree with him."

"Please don't accuse me of shooting John." She met my eye, steadily, almost imploringly. "I wouldn't do that. That would never be within the call of duty."

I closed my eyes. A moment later the television upstairs was clicked off. A rasping, hacking cough echoed, then stopped. Outside somewhere, a man continued his wolfish howling.

I said, "Danny tried to explain his suicide to me, when he was dying in the bathtub. How he had nothing left."

"Except his cause and the loyalty of his friends,"

Barbara said quietly. ''I'm the one who leaked it, you know, that John was an agent. I did it carefully, through Keith. I told Keith I saw John coming out of the bureau office in the Federal Building. I knew Keith would figure out a way to prove the worst—he was so jealous of John's relationship with Dan. I also knew Keith wouldn't give me credit for the tip. That's not his style.''

''Why did you do it?''

''I'd wasted a month already—there's nothing illegal or even very threatening going on at the Clearinghouse. But I did find out John couldn't be trusted—he was completely in Danny's pocket. I even wondered if they were having a love affair, although there was nothing in either of their files indicating homosexual tendencies. Anyway, I recommended firing John. And my orders were to discredit him with the Clearinghouse people— have him cast out so he wouldn't discuss our operations with them.''

I opened my eyes. Barbara sat forward, watching me, obviously wanting me to understand. As one career woman to another?

''So you blew the whistle on John.''

''It's not that I wanted to hurt Dan Crosetti. Really.''

In a way, it was the saddest possible epitaph. Danny had posed no threat to the FBI; its agents could afford to be kind.

She continued, ''We're not the same bureau we were under Mr. Hoover. We're more realistic in our appraisals. Honestly.''

I replayed what Danny had told me through his bathroom door. I relived his litany—trucks running over him on government orders and with court approval, disability checks stopped, four and a half years of jail time. Eighteen years of agony and poverty and restriction coming to a head when he learned that his friend was a government agent.

But there was one thing Dan Crosetti hadn't said—and hadn't denied.

"Did he really kill John Lefevre? Did he really?" I could still hear Danny's fury and outrage and pain as he explained why he'd purchased the rifle.

"Laura, believe me, I wish I'd never leaked the information."

The government had mown Dan Crosetti down again. And this time it seemed personal—not just political, not just economic. He couldn't take it. He struck back. He killed John Lefevre.

My God. He killed John Lefevre.

Barbara's voice clotted with emotion. "I never—none of us ever thought Crosetti would—"

I stared at her. The story had the awful ring of familiarity. I'd put Wallace Bean out on the streets three years ago, and three people ended up dead. Dead because I'd done my job right.

We were a tidy, competent pair, Barbara Nottata and I. Building our careers on fresh graves.

"You moved the crutches?"

"Yes. I came here to tell Danny. I wanted him to know I was an FBI agent—that I'd betrayed John because John had turned against the bureau."

"Confession being good for the soul?"

Her chin crinkled. "For what it was worth, I wanted Danny to know that John was his friend. Sincerely."

"You let Dan kill himself."

"The alternative was federal penitentiary. I just—" She looked away, scarlet-cheeked, tiny beads of perspiration on her upper lip.

"You let him—"

"I let him make his own decision! It was clearly what he planned to do anyway. I just wanted him to know—" She squirmed on the hard chair. "I took the crutches away."

"Why?"

"An accommodation. A way for me to feel less guilty."

"Why did you take them away?"

"So you'd—" She blinked at me. "I thought you could—"

I jumped to my feet. Oh Lord, how could she? "You wanted to confuse things. So I'd kick up some dust."

"For Danny's sake. So there would be some doubt. So people—people who were so inclined—could keep thinking of him as a martyr." Her eyes were large and luminous.

I took a few quick strides across the room. Stood over her, my fingers stiff with the desire to slap her.

I'd made a fool of myself on network television. I'd watched my career liquefy like quicksand.

She looked up at me, her face as damp and rapturous as Saint Joan's. "I owed it to Dan Crosetti. If the bureau finds out, they'll crucify me, but I don't care. I had to do it."

I turned away. Two federal agents had, in varying degrees, embarrassed the government for Danny's sake. It was certainly a testament.

But it didn't keep me from feeling like the cat with singed paws.

I paced across the room. Turned back to the woman whose belated scruples had cost me so much. "What are you looking for now? What were you looking for in my office?"

She shook her head. "That wasn't me. Last night at your office—that wasn't me."

I felt my face tighten into a scowl. Did I believe her? "Why are we here now? You said Hal called."

"I'm sorry—I needed to talk to you. I got the information about your cousin from the civic-center office. They accessed an all-points bulletin." She looked a little sick. "You're very close to Hal Di Palma, aren't you? Not just related?"

I took several deep breaths. Mustn't fall to pieces before I knew— "So what are we doing here?"

She pressed her lips together, squeezed her eyes shut. A tear ran down each cheek. "I've been reassigned. To New Bedford, Massachusetts." Her eyes opened. "I leave in the morning."

A fucking good-bye confession? What the hell for?

"If your detective continues investigating, he'll realize who I am."

"So you're telling me because I'd have found out anyway."

"I thought if I told you here, at Danny's house, you'd understand—"

"Jesus." I backed away. "An FBI agent conspiring to make a martyr out of someone who—"

"I know." She flinched. "He killed someone. And I guess you'd be well within your rights to make that public information."

"Oh Jesus." I paced awhile longer, looking at Danny's sad odds and ends of furniture, at the idealism weeping from his walls.

Barbara Nottata was correct. If I said nothing, the conspiracy theories would flourish. There would always be those who thought Danny had been murdered; or that he'd killed himself as a result of persecution, not guilt.

I'd thought so myself. I'd considered Danny a martyr. I was startled to find I still did.

But others wouldn't. They wouldn't care how far Danny had been pushed.

"I told Danny who I was, and—" Barbara wiped her tears away. "And I told him John wanted to leave the bureau. I mean, it was my fault Danny felt so betrayed. I just wanted him to know— It must have been some comfort to know John really did care about him. Don't you think?"

"Yes." The syllable was pulled out of me by the sheer force of Barbara's desire to hear it.

"I wish I knew I'd done the right thing." She gnawed her lip again. "Either way, Danny would have killed himself for killing John. At the Clearinghouse that afternoon, he made it plain. I could tell by the way he acted—like part of him had faded away already. Later, I told everyone Danny had decided to go underground, but that wasn't true."

Telling the truth wouldn't bring John Lefevre back. It might give me the satisfaction of screwing up Barbara's career as she'd helped screw up mine; it even make the FBI look bad, for a while. had taken his guilt to the grave to avoid I didn't know what that said about a friend, and that you keep a fr can.

"And what could I do to raised an imploring hand. "I n the right to try? I followed hi everything. He didn't say a wo bath. Awhile later, I followed hin away. Danny didn't even seem to notice. He was sitting there holding a razor blade, just sitting there holding it. He hadn't done it yet, but he was already—'' She groped for the right word.

I thought of my last conversation with Dan Crosetti, and I knew what the word was. "He was already gone."

"I got back to the Clearinghouse right before you came."

"And the whole time we talked, you knew Danny was—"

"Yes." Tears streaked her now-composed face; she looked like a weeping statue. "I knew he was gone."

33

I STOOD AT Danny's front window, watching through broken glass and steel bars as Barbara's little Colt pulled away from the curb.

Tonight she would vanish from Bay Area activism as suddenly as she'd appeared, pleading homesickness and a desire to reconcile with her fictional husband.

Anything else that might happen depended on me. Barbara Nottata knew it and I knew it. She didn't argue when I told her I'd rather call a cab than ride with her. Poised again and thoroughly professional, she knew when to talk and when not to.

I let the bedsheet curtain fall closed. I turned back to the thumbtack-riddled walls, the dusty squalor, the stacked papers.

It was quiet now. No television upstairs, no howling man, no passers-by, no night traffic. Hunters Point was as silent as a vast, decaying museum.

I walked slowly through the living room. Barbara

Nottata had risked censure and unemployment to let me know how deeply Dan Crosetti affected her. She was counting on my loyalty to Danny. Counting on me to help cleanse his tarnished image.

I stepped into the plank-floor hallway, looking again at the bathroom door.

"Danny?" I touched the cold porcelain doorknob. "I'm so sorry. So sorry you got pushed so far."

I closed my eyes, gripping the knob. I listened to a dead voice through the closed door.

I knew the world wept for victims, with little pity to spare on perpetrators. I knew I'd been cynical in my defense of killers. But wouldn't people—some people— see where the lines blurred? See the painful shades of gray?

My answer came in the form of a jingle I'd memorized a few hours earlier: *Susan Yen, again. Nine eight nine, ten ten.*

I'd gone public. I'd told the world Dan Crosetti was innocent.

The truth was much sadder and more complicated than that.

34

Susan Yen wore red again. Her glossy hair was in a French braid, not free and flowing as it had been during the deputy DA's press conference. But she still had the look of an oracle, of someone beholding greater drama than the ordinary eye can observe.

And it was no ordinary eye she trained on me that night. It was the glinting black lens of a minicamera, assisted by a spotlight facing Dan Crosetti's chair.

She spoke calmly. "I'll begin with an introduction—similar to what we'll voice over at the studio—and then segue to you with a very general question, allowing you to do most of the talking."

I remembered her voice from an interview eighteen months ago, after the law-school-murders verdict. I couldn't recall why I'd granted Susan Yen an interview then; I hadn't granted many. And Channel 33 was small potatoes, relying too heavily on "community programming" and sixties sitcoms. Maybe some moments are so important they can reach backward in time to arrange themselves.

For me, it was that kind of moment. I sat very straight in Dan Crosetti's chair. I didn't care how I looked and I didn't care what kind of image I projected. My credibility did not depend on anything external, tonight. People would feel the justice of my words, or they wouldn't. I could only hope and explain.

Susan Yen clicked a button, and the room filled with the soft hum of a camera. She said, "Laura Di Palma is a well-known criminal lawyer who has built a reputation for getting lenient sentences for guilty clients. Twelve days ago, she was hired to represent Daniel Crosetti, a local peace activist accused of murdering purported fellow activist John Lefevre. Crosetti was accused of purchasing a rifle and shooting John Lefevre when he learned that Lefevre was actually an FBI agent. Three days ago, Crosetti, out on bail, committed suicide. I am sitting now in Daniel Crosetti's living room with Attorney Di Palma. Ms. Di Palma, can you give us your thoughts on what's happened?"

I let my gaze waver from the lens to the unobscured half of the reporter's face. She watched me with the vibrant hopefulness I'd sensed in Inspector Kelly before I signed my statement.

Daniel Crosetti had committed himself to blocking a road, and he'd left blood and bone there. He'd committed himself to ideals that cost him every hope of affluence and ease.

I looked at the camera eye again, and committed myself to the plain truth. "Daniel Crosetti killed John Lefevre. I want to try to explain why."

35

I FIT THE key into my downstairs lock, inhaling mentholated wind. Eucalyptus trees rustled, a couple down the street kissed under a porch light, a garage door opened to reveal a shiny green Jaguar, a man in a Stanford sweatshirt jogged bouncily along the curb.

For the first time in days, security and familiarity made me feel thankful rather than guilty.

I opened the downstairs door and stepped into a hallway of polished parquet. I heard Susan Yen drive away.

I climbed up to my flat and opened the door.

The living room was dark, but not empty. A silhouette blocked the moonlight through my bay window.

The shadow stirred.

"Sandy?"

"Yuh. Nottata's a federal agent, isn't she?"

"Yes." I crossed to the couch, leaving the lights off. The darkness was soothing.

"I've been hanging around here thinking, Laura.

About the look of that woman, about her nice bureau-
cratic little car. Thinking if she's a white shirt then a
couple of things make sense.''

"She leaked the information that Lefevre was a fed.
She hinted it to Asimov, and let him take 'credit' for
the information.''

"So Lefevre was on his way out?''

"He was going to be fired—he'd gotten too close to
Crosetti. The FBI wanted to discredit him with the
Clearinghouse people first.''

"And the G-lady felt bad when Crosetti reacted by
killing Lefevre.''

"Yes.''

A slow exhalation. "Women.''

I let the word hang in the air, another index of our
differences. Today I'd seen Sandy's contempt for pacifists; glimpsed genuine anger in his staged goading of
Asimov. I hadn't thought about Sandy's politics before;
it had been years since I'd considered anyone's politics
important.

"She moved Danny's crutches. She wanted people to
be able to think Danny'd been murdered—set up all the
way. People who wanted to think so anyway, who
wanted to see him as a martyr. She says she did it for
Danny.''

"A little late to be worrying about Crosetti.''

"I think so, too. I told Channel 33 the truth.''

He turned his back on me, looking out the window
at moonlit gum trees and hilly fairways. "Okay.''

"Nottata says she had nothing to do with Doron
White; that it wasn't her in my office. I believe her.''

"It was Asimov.''

"Jesus Christ, Sandy.'' Hadn't we already danced this
dance? Already slandered, assaulted, and battered the man?

"Has to be Asimov," Sandy repeated.

"I know you don't like him, but—"

"Oh, spare me!" He turned back around, striding out of his alcove and dropping to a squat in front of me.

"Can't you put this bleeding-heart business out of your mind for a second, Laura? Give me credit for what I know how to do, which is think about this kind of—" A deep sigh.

I could see Sandy's long face in shades of black and moonlit gray, twitching with chagrin.

"Why Asimov?"

"Crosetti said he came to your house the night you bailed him out. That he talked to Hal here."

"Yes."

"So who drove him?"

"For all we know he took a cab." I relaxed against the cushions of the couch. God, I was tired.

Sandy smoothed my hair. "Suppose Asimov did drive Crosetti here that night. Crosetti wanted to tell you about the rifle—maybe tell you everything. But he didn't want Asimov to hear. Too embarrassing, right?"

"Yes." Danny found it embarrassing, all right.

"So"—Sandy leaned forward as if proximity would strengthen his argument—"he asks Asimov to wait in the car."

We stared at one another. I felt dehydrated and achy. I didn't see what the hell difference it made whether Asimov was waiting in the car that night.

"What's Asimov supposed to think?" Sandy said impatiently.

"About what?"

"He's going to think Crosetti gave you something— maybe something incriminating. For safekeeping."

"What kind of thing?"

Sandy settled himself on the floor, knees sticking up like a daddy-longlegs. "I don't know."

I closed my eyes. "Go home, Sandy. I'm beat."

He slid his hand over mine, turning my palm up.

I knew what he was going to do. It had been three years since he'd kissed my palm, but I knew. I yanked my hand away.

"Let me stay," he said softly.

I closed my eyes, willing what remained of my strength into my voice. "Go home."

36

I WAS STILL on the couch, curled into a tight, limb-numbing ball. The room was dark—darker than when Sandy left. I wasn't sure what had waked me. I started to stretch my cramped legs when I heard a sound.

It was wind. Wind unmuffled by the curtains I'd forgotten to close. Wind that was too loud. Wind I could feel and smell, as well as hear.

I sat up cautiously, feeling cold air stir my hair and sting my cheeks. Somewhere a window was open.

Had Sandy opened a window?

I was completely, suddenly awake. I turned toward the bay windows. Yes, one of them was open. Sandy certainly hadn't done that.

I stood quickly, feeling a little nauseous. I wanted to call out, to find out if I was alone. I restrained the impulse.

I tiptoed to the window. If it was opened from the outside, opened while I slept, there might still be an intruder in the apartment. Someone who assumed, given the dark rooms and open curtains, that the apartment was empty. Someone who hadn't noticed me curled into a ball behind the plump sofa arm.

I looked out the window. The moon was cushioned in night fog, and every crackle of twigs, every stirring of leaves seemed threatening.

At first I didn't see the ladder. I reached out and felt for it. When my fingers encountered cold grooved aluminum, I heard myself moan.

Then I heard a noise behind me somewhere; in the bedroom, probably. I could see a glimmer of light on the trees outside the bedroom window. Someone in there with a flashlight.

The night air was as chill as lake water. I felt my skin shrink into gooseflesh.

Suddenly the light on the leaves vanished. I looked over my shoulder and saw a bright path on the Persian runner of my hallway.

No time to run across the living room to the front door. With the heel of my hand, I tested the ladder.

I hoisted my leg over the window sill. The wobbling glow of flashlight moved through the hall.

I didn't have time to be quiet. I found a rung with one foot as I swung the other leg out the window.

From the corridor, a startled epithet. Suddenly the beam of light hit me in the eyes, dazzling me.

Blinded, I gripped the fog-slick metal and clambered, fell, and slid down the rungs, gasping and barking my shins. Before I reached bottom, I lost my footing completely. I fell the remaining five feet, with the ladder arcing down toward me.

I raised my forearms to ward off the metal. As I looked up, the flashlight was shined into my face again, and I caught a glimpse of hands, someone else's hands, knocking away the falling ladder. Suddenly, I was yanked out of the circle of light.

My right knee and hand were scraped across the gravel verge between my building and the concrete alley. Rough fingers gripped my left arm and my shoulder, dragging me, hoisting me, pulling me across the alley. I was too scared to fight; too stunned to know if I was being kidnapped or saved.

My captor and I stumbled against the waist-high stone wall bordering the Presidio fairways. The flashlight found us again, but before I could look at my captor, my face was full of his sweater, his hands grabbed my shoulders, and I was knocked backward over the wall.

I landed with a painful jolt to the ribcage, a jarring of jaw and shoulder. To the extent that I could see at all, I saw beads of fog glistening around me. The flashlight had tracked my fall.

Someone, the man with the sweater, landed beside me, his leg knocking my face into the damp grass, choking me with dirt and twigs.

The man rolled toward the wall, pulling and yanking me toward him. When I coughed the dirt out of my mouth and eyes, I could see that we were in the shadow of the stone wall. The distant flashlight wavered dimly over the grass beyond us, searching.

In the instant before he spoke, I knew. Knew from cues that hadn't had a chance to register before.

He was gasping for breath. But as snide as ever. "I see you've been keeping out of trouble."

"Hal!"

37

I DIDN'T CARE who the hell was in my apartment, or what his plans might be. If he wanted something, he was welcome to it. If he wanted to come outside and get me, fine. But he'd have to pull me off Hal.

At that moment, my worst problem seemed to be the five-day growth on Hal's chin.

Hal pulled back a little, one arm still locked around me, the other stroking my hair. "So who's after you now?"

"I have no idea."

"Think we should run?" he murmured.

"Don't make me think."

"Would I do that to you?" His tone wasn't light; he didn't do light very well. "I'm a little ripe."

"I don't care."

I stood over a trapdoor of disillusionment and I clung to Hal. Clung to the moment. In the darkness, I could pretend he was the same as ever. I could pretend he looked at me like I mattered in a way nothing else did. In the cold light of wherever we went next, I would probably find a man still crippled in body and attitude.

"I don't suppose you know if your friend has a gun?"

"No." Hal's sweater was scratchy with twigs, the skin of his neck rough and scraped and clammy cold. "Are you all right, Hal?"

A derisive snicker. "Sure. Just swell."

I choked back a flood of sympathy and apology. What good would it do?

"I think maybe we should make tracks, Laura. Your boogie man's not going to come out the back—not with the ladder down. We should go around front. See if he's gone."

He rose, extending his right hand. I took it, aware that the fingers closed around mine. Not tightly, but they did close.

"Want to be boring and go through the gate this time?"

Hal began walking toward an opening in the wall. I felt a sick pang. His right leg dragged.

A streetlamp above the gate glowed an eerie, fog-dimmed orange. Sickle-shaped eucalyptus leaves blew around it, casting distorted, dancing shadows. As if through a dim pool, I watched Hal walk. From half a pace behind him I watched, knowing from the tense lift of his shoulders that he knew I watched. The ground he covered was uneven and leaf-strewn, but it might as well have been the rehabilitation-center floor.

He would always be conscious of it. And of me, watching for signs of improvement.

Directly under the streetlamp, he turned to face me.

"Phantom of the opera," he said.

I touched the right side of his face. The cheek seemed abnormally hollow, the corner of the mouth unnaturally fixed. His right eyelid drooped slightly.

But confusion and anxiety no longer twisted the left side of his face. Resentment no longer dulled his eyes.

"You're a lot better," I said.

His smile betrayed a lack of elasticity on the right side of his face. "Better than what?"

His hair was wild, his skin smeared, his sweater snagged and stained.

Tears spilled down my cheeks. "Where were you, Hal? I almost went nuts."

"I called," he pointed out. "Twice. So you'd know I wasn't . . ."

I looked up at him, speechless. Did he really believe those calls had been a comfort?

"And I went to your office." A frown that made him look ten years older. "Thinking you'd be there."

I pushed Doron White out of my mind. Time enough later. "Where have you been staying?"

"Right here. Life on the links."

"The Presidio?" Behind my apartment? "Outside?"

"Yeah. Watching your window from the trees. Thinking."

I slid my arms around his waist. Had he proved to himself he could still live in devil-may-care transience? Live without me?

"I guess I came to the obvious conclusion." His voice was weary. "I'm too fucking old for this, Laura."

I kept my arms tightly around him.

"I've gotten soft, I guess. I can't take it anymore— the cold, the hard ground, the scrounging—it's just too hard."

I thought of Dan Crosetti and the cross-country peace march he'd been too old and too sick to tackle.

Hal buried his face in my hair. "From one day to the next"—his voice was muffled; not enough to disguise the pain—"one day to the next, I got old."

So he wasn't the man he used to be. Not so devil-may-care.

"Don't cry to me, Hal. I didn't like that part of you, anyway."

"That's the good news." He gripped me more tightly.

He stepped back, keeping one arm around my shoulder. "I should probably get a fucking cane. I've been using branches."

We walked slowly toward the side of the house. Hal leaned on me, obviously weary and winded.

"I got fired. Doron fired me."

Silence.

When we reached the front porch, he said, "You okay? About the job?"

"I don't know. They might have rehired me if I'd toed the line." Kept myself out of the public eye for a while; off the Channel 33 news. "I guess it was my call. My choice."

"What are you going to do?"

"Slow boat to Alaska?"

I tried the apartment-house door. Locked, of course.

"Maybe the boogie man's still up there." Hal pressed the button labeled Apartment 2. "Maybe he'll buzz us in." Hal smiled, a somewhat twisted smile, but not lacking in charm.

And sure enough, a second later, a buzzer sounded, indicating that the door had been electronically unlocked.

"Hospitable fellow," Hal observed. "You feeling brave?"

"Yes."

He held the door open for me. "Then you go first."

38

In his left hand, Mark Bresenzcy gripped a hand-blown glass of water. Tendrils of blond hair fell over his pale cheeks, and his narrow shoulders sagged. For the first time all night my lamps were lit and my curtains were drawn.

Bresenzcy squirmed uncomfortably in the down chair. I sat on the floor beside Hal, wishing Bresenzcy would stop apologizing and get on with it. I wanted to be alone with Hal.

I summed up, trying to hurry him along: "Asimov told you he'd driven Danny to my apartment late one night. And that he thought Danny had given me something for safekeeping." Sandy had been right on both counts, though not in his conclusion.

Bresenzcy nodded miserably.

"So presumably you're the one who was at my office looking through my desk—"

"I'm sorry." Sweat beaded on Bresenzcy's forehead,

capturing wisps of hair. "You sent me in to meet your clerks the day Keith and Barbara and I came to your office. One of them let me back in later. I told her you wanted me to do some more research."

The law clerks. Sandy had talked to the firm's word processors and its associates. We hadn't thought of the clerks.

"I was sitting at your desk, and that man—Mr. White—came in and started ranting. I didn't mean to hurt him, honestly! I tried to run out of there, but he grabbed my sweater. All I did was tap him, just a couple of light—"

"And Doron fell down and hit the chair and had a heart attack."

"What?" Beside me Hal stiffened. "Doron White had a heart attack?"

"He's dead."

"I just took the bar exam again this summer," Bresenzcy pleaded softly. "And I think I passed it this time. So the State Bar will be investigating me . . . to certify me fit to practice."

I closed my eyes, leaning my head on Hal's shoulder. He did smell ripe: unbathed, mossy, with a faint overlay of hospital disinfectant.

Doron White's wife, for all I knew, loved Doron as deeply as I loved Hal. If I kept Bresenzcy's secret, she would never know what had happened to her husband. She would go through life wondering if Doron had been attacked by a colleague, by someone who understood and intended the consequences.

A few days without Hal had shown me the ravages of uncertainty. I couldn't help Bresenzcy. In the morning, I would call Inspector Krisbaum.

I said, "What you were looking for—it's something you don't want the State Bar to know about?"

A blush crept up Bresenzcy's cheeks. "Danny and I acquired some information in a way that wasn't strictly—I mean, it was morally correct, but not strictly—"

"Not strictly legal. Involving Nuclear Watch?"

He nodded.

"I have bad news for you. The FBI already has the information." Why else would Barbara Nottata lie so elaborately about the missing Nuclear Watch map?

Bresenzcy set the water glass down abruptly, almost missing the end table.

I continued, "The good news is the FBI probably won't prosecute. It's sticky, what they were doing at the Clearinghouse." One agent they distrusted and a second agent there to spy on him. Both agents undergoing political conversions, of sorts. The FBI would stonewall. It wouldn't fuel the fire with minor arrests. "They'll just stick the information into your file."

Bresenzcy seemed to wilt. "But the State Bar—"

"Will see the file. And probably won't certify you to practice."

Any other day, I'd have felt a great deal sorrier for Mark Bresenzcy. Today I wouldn't wish the practice of law on anyone.

My attitude startled me. I'd always been high on my profession. I must have been, to lavish all my energy on it.

I buried my face in Hal's sweater. I'd spoken in jest earlier, but maybe it wasn't such a bad idea. Maybe a slow boat to Alaska was just what I needed. We needed.

Hal put his arms around me.

I heard him say to Bresenzcy, "Go away. Take your fucking ladder with you."

I heard the scrape of Bresenzcy's shoes. Halting footsteps. Heard him pause at the door before he left.

Hal slipped a hand under my chin and tilted my face toward his. "Jesus, you've had a rotten week."

I nodded.

He moistened his lips and kissed me. "Let me go clean up."

I watched him stand. "Your phone message—you said you were going after Crosetti the night you had your— the night you got sick. Why?"

Hal winced. "I talked to Crosetti when he came by here that night. He was falling apart. I thought he might—I thought he needed to be with someone who wouldn't act disappointed in him."

"What happened then? What happened to you?" I looked at him through a blur of tears, remembering the way I'd found him, mumbling unintelligibly, trying to drag himself to the door.

His face went blank. Hard. Hating the memory of his helplessness?

"A stroke, I guess. Isn't that what they said at the hospital?" He turned away.

A minute later, I heard the shower. I gave him five minutes before I joined him.

EPILOGUE

Hal Di Palma sat alone in the dark room. He didn't think Laura would awaken any time soon, but as a precaution, he'd closed the bedroom door before limping into the living room.

He ached, less so on the right side of his body than the left, but all over. The increasing bilateralism was comforting. And the pain was nothing compared to the last few days. The last few days had been devastating, physically and emotionally.

He blamed one man for it. For what had happened, and for what would continue to happen: the right-arm weakness, the sinister-looking rigidity of his face, the cane he would have to adopt. He felt that he'd been transformed from a young man to an old man from one moment to the next.

And he remembered the moment. The exact moment.

As if on cue, he heard the click of a key in the front-door lock. The door swung quietly open. Against the bright light of the stairwell a lean silhouette.

The figure stepped in, closing the door softly behind itself.

Hal said, "I thought you might drop by."

"Di Palma! Jesus! Where'd you—" Sandy Arkelett took a stumbling step backward.

Hal rose, clicking on the reading lamp beside his chair. "Hoping I'd stay gone?"

Sandy recovered his balance, slipped his hands into his trouser pockets. He stood there, concentrating, looking Di Palma over.

Hal endured the scrutiny, knowing well what the other man saw. A face that was haggard and sunken on one side. A body that listed to the left, favoring the good leg. But also a man who was clean and comfortable. A man who'd been back for a while, and intended to remain.

He said, "Toss over your key, Arkelett."

Sandy pulled the key out of his pocket and tossed it. It hit Hal's jeans, sliding down to his bare foot.

"Look, Di Palma, I'm sorry. I was so pissed off I couldn't see straight. The way you treat her—"

"She can take it!" Remorse chilled him. But it was nothing he would discuss with this man.

"I never would have done it if I'd known you were going to blow a fuse." Sandy tapped his temple. "Not in a million years. I've been feeling like a worm."

"But you didn't tell her you decked me."

A sound between a moan and a laugh. "Tell her I stopped by for the scoop on Crosetti and ended up sending you to the hospital? She'd have hated me for life."

Hal rubbed the spot where his neck met his skull. It

had been a hell of a chop, delivered with the force of jealous anger. "You left me lying there."

"I didn't know how bad it was. I just thought you were down."

The men looked at one another.

"You didn't tell her either. Why not?"

Hal crossed his arms over his chest. "She likes working with you. And her work's important to her."

Arkelett frowned at his hand as if considering extending it. But Di Palma's arms were still crossed.

The detective turned and left.